Harvest Tales
& Midnight Revels

Stories for the Waning of the Year

Harvest Tales
& Midnight Revels

Stories for the Waning of the Year

Edited by Michael Mayhew   Illustrated by Mona Caron

Bald Mountain Books
San Francisco 1998

*To the first storyteller,
who dared to wonder at the world.*

Acknowledgments

A project of this scope does not see the light of day without the input and support (and encouragement and handholding, etc.) of numerous people. Bald Mountain Books is grateful to all who helped us to realize the goal of bringing this, our first publication, to readers everywhere. We are particularly grateful to Walter Mayes, advisor extraordinaire, who tried valiantly to dissuade us from this project and, when he saw our determination, gave us consistently helpful advice and contacts; Melissa Mytinger, publicist, whose efforts on our behalf continued to bear fruit throughout her own tribulations; our families and friends, who allowed us this dream without inhibition.

Contents

Harvest Tales
& Midnight Revels

Stories for the Waning of the Year

INTRODUCTION

by Michael Mayhew

All Hallow's Eve, The Witches' Sabbath, El Día
de los Muertos, Carnival of the Souls, Samhain...

By my third year of college, I knew something was missing. The feeling had been tickling at me for a while and then, on Halloween night, 1983, it crystallized.

Early evening, but chill. I was walking home from class, hands jammed into my jacket pockets to keep warm. The moon dodged in and out of scudding clouds. Leaves scurried along the sidewalk in little swirls. A perfect Halloween, really.

But there were no trick-or-treaters.

Not for the whole length of the block. Empty. Silent. Dead. Except...a father and his two kids: a tiny superhero and a tinier princess and Dad, with his flashlight, looking like the man who has gone to a PTA meeting on the wrong night. I gave him a little wave, and he managed a wry smile—a sort of "I know I look silly" smile. Then he hurried the kids along. There were few houses to stop at anyway. Most of the lights were out.

It was seven o' clock on Halloween night and nobody seemed to care.

Halloween! Witches and monsters and candy and wind! Leaves in the gutter and dust devils! Sweaters and cinnamon, new crisp apples and pumpkin guts!

And, flavoring all of this, a sweet-sad melancholy. Halloween is about the death of things, and even as a child I could feel it. Halloween says flowers fade, friendships diminish, lovers depart...and people die. Halloween is an acknowledgement of death and a defiance of it all in one; a mad, merry *danse macabre*, a long deep stare into the void, a shout to the infinite, "You may get me someday, but tonight I am alive!"

What had become of all that?

Halloween was always my favorite holiday when I was young. I loved trick-or-treating and later, when I was in high school, throwing elaborate parties with costumes, lighting effects and headstones on the lawn. But now, here I was in college and the whole thing seemed to have died. And it wasn't just that there weren't any trick-or-treaters in my college neighborhood. That bothered me, but on the other hand I certainly didn't want to do that anymore, nor any of the other things that I had done on Halloween as a kid.

Something was missing.

The problem, then and now, is that there isn't really any way for adults to celebrate Halloween. Sure, people throw costume parties, and those are fun, but the core of the holiday gets lost. Whatever magical shivers we get as children by tramping about in the night don't translate into drinks in the living room.

Is Halloween just a children's holiday? Many people think so. But that wasn't always the case. The changing light of winter's approach used to signal the death of the world; now it means little more than driving home in the dark.

What is Halloween?

And in the more recent resurgence of commercial interest in the holiday—the "Halloween stores" that crop up in malls each year around mid-September, the costumes and greeting cards and beer campaigns, ringing up millions of dollars of business annually—the question becomes even more acute.

What is Halloween?

Forget, for the moment, the issue of what the holiday has been—its history and all. The question at hand is what is it now, to us, in our world, at the end of the twentieth century?

Walking home that night, many years ago, all I knew was that something had gone missing and I wanted it back. I didn't yet know what the question was but, almost inadvertently, I went about asking it.

I have always had the good fortune to have a lot of extremely creative friends. I set about with them to find adult ways to celebrate Halloween and find its core. One year we all went to an old cemetery and drank cheap champagne amongst the headstones. Another time someone found a haunted turn-of-the-century mansion and we waltzed all night in the crumbling courtyard.

But the idea that stuck was ghost story parties.

The notion is as old as the first cook fire: a group of people gather together to feast and tell stories. One such gathering in the nineteenth century gave rise to Mary Shelley's *Frankenstein*. Our parties were less ambitious: guests were invited to bring a potluck dish and an original story. The story had to relate to Halloween in some way—exactly what way was up to the writer.

And that last part was what made all the difference. The rules for what type of story could be brought and read were meant to encourage people to bring something. It's hard enough to get busy, talented people to write a story just for a party game; I didn't want someone to decide his or her story wouldn't "fit" and not bring it. But what happened, because the rules were so vague, was that each story became part of a larger conversation.

"What is Halloween?" became the starting point for over eighty stories written over the course of ten years. Eighty answers to the same question. Eighty perspectives on what that ancient, pagan tradition meant to creative people living in today's urban landscape.

And as the story party evolved over the years, the event itself became part of the dialogue. The vagueness of my instructions to writers was perhaps a reflection of the broader vague meaning the holiday holds for most adults. Turns out that Halloween can be whatever you want it to be.

Halloween has no rules. Unlike, say, Christmas, no relative's feelings will be hurt if you decide to spend Halloween with your mother's side of the family this year. Or your father's. No one will look askance if you serve duck (or ice cream, or fish sticks) on Halloween night. You can throw a costume party. You can hand out candy. You can dance around a bonfire in blue paint. You can read stories. There are no rules.

If I could share only one thing about what we did and learned over ten years of story parties it would be this: the Halloween that shrieked with glee when you were eight is still out there, only now it murmurs to itself in the dead of night, and if you listen for it, out by the trees when the late afternoon light is just so, you will find that it offers a few choice blessings to those who enjoy the shivers enough to play in the dark. It's a matter of training your ears.

But I have more to share with you. Lots more. A bookful of stories, for one thing. And some advice on how to start your own story parties as well.

What follows is a collection of the very best work from those ten years of story parties, written by a very special group of friends—writers, artists, musicians and filmmakers.

All the tales were read aloud on or near Halloween night, with a fire on the hearth and warm mugs of Irish Coffee to keep the chill at bay.

This book is our way of sharing one type of Halloween geared specifically toward adults—one that has mostly to do with food and friends, stories and laughter, wind and leaves, October and the shivers.

Aside from that, there are only two things you should know: 1) The stories in this book are very eclectic. Each author had his own perspective on Halloween, and the results go all over the stylistic map, from Gothic horror to absurdist comedy of manners, from wistful reminiscence to cyberpunk; and 2) THIS IS NOT A CHILDREN'S BOOK. A few of these stories are appropriate to read to children, but the majority of them are too dark and too explicit for children. Please do not give this to a child to read unsupervised. This book is about creating a Halloween for adults to enjoy.

So turn down the lights, get a mug of whatever you like to drink to keep the chill off your bones, and have a haunted Halloween. I hope your skies are full of leaves. I hope your attic is full of creaks.

— Michael Mayhew
Los Angeles, 1998

Now is the time
when the veil between worlds
is thinnest

Michael Mayhew

Carrion Bird

from
1993
What is Halloween?
Monsters, Vampires, Creatures of the Night.
The stories at our parties featured all of these in spades over the years, although usually only one or two "monster" stories would show up at any given party. Some years, though, without prior agreement, most of the stories would coalesce around a single theme—as if all the authors were resonating in tune with a broader zeitgeist.

Nineteen ninety-three was the year of erotic love stories. Most of the stories that year touched upon themes of love or sex or both. "Carrion Bird" was no exception.

But I thought I was being different.

"Carrion Bird" was written in response to a small press magazine that published only "erotic vampire" stories. I was tickled by the notion that a magazine would have such a narrow focus. What on Earth was there left to say about vampires? Particularly after Anne Rice, what erotic thing was there to say?

The thought gnawed at me, and shortly thereafter I began to write this eccentric love story, which was finished just in time for the party.

Then, during the course of the readings, I was amused to discover that almost every writer had similar things on their minds.

What is Halloween?
Sometimes it's sex.

Carrion Bird

by Michael Mayhew

She sits at the bar like a half-filled burlap sack, sipping generic Chardonnay. Nobody sees the trembling in her fingers. Not even the bartender. Nor does anyone notice that the dress she wears is a new one. Not their fault; the dress is plain.

They do not see how afraid she is, how lonely she is, how desperate she is. They do not see that for her this drink is a step in a ritual.

All they see is a fat lady drinking wine.

Slowly. Too goddamned slowly. If she doesn't finish and leave soon I'm screwed. Every vulture for miles is gonna spot her juicy body flailing on the emotional plains and not one of them'll give a damn that I found her three weeks ago.

Come on, lady. Let's go.

Wouldn't you know my melancholy little wildebeest would set her plump heart on a "last drink." This plan of hers could go very badly for me.

She's sipping. She wants to be noticed. She wants to be approached. Nobody can see it. How could they? She's wrapped around her glass like a child wrapped around her mother's leg. Hardly the person to strike up a conversation with.

No vampires yet. Chug-a-lug, lady, down the hatch.

At last she finishes her wine, pays, and leaves the bar. I follow like black mercury flowing across the floor.

Better.

You have to understand it's not about blood. If it was about blood then hunting would be easy. But blood is not especially nourishing. *Life* is nourishing, but that's the trick. Stealing life is very hard.

The best prey are drunks and junkies. They're easiest and believe me, easy counts. Easy being a relative term— maybe one in a hundred alcoholics has the right combination of self-destructiveness and self-pity to let himself get eaten.

Sometimes you can pick up a good meal at a nursing home but it's harder than you'd think. Most old people have a tenacious grip on life. Those that don't haven't much worth stealing.

Then there are the lonelies. Hard work, those. You have to put a lot of hours in at the local high school before you find the one kid who's gonna hang himself. And then he might change his mind, find Jesus, get High on Life and there goes dinner.

But that's also the advantage. The ratio of predator to prey is very favorable with lonelies.

I am a carrion bird, and I feed on the weak.

She drives a nondescript Japanese econobox, the color of dust on the horizon. I sit beside her in the passenger seat, but do not allow her to see me. She senses me, though. Her eyes dart and she has trouble getting the key into the ignition, but she attributes this to her own nervousness about her itinerary.

Or perhaps she does understand but has ceased caring. No one is ever surprised to see me. (Is a crippled zebra surprised to see hyenas arrive? No. Certainly dismayed, but never surprised.)

She arrives at a revival theatre—the last one in the city, and likely to close due to competition from video. Tonight they are showing *To Catch A Thief*, with Cary Grant and Grace Kelly. My prey buys herself a ticket, and then at the candy counter buys a SuperSaver tub of popcorn, some Junior Mints, a box of Red Vines, a Hershey Bar, and a large Coke. There are two kids working the candy counter. The one who takes her order has purple hair and winks to the other one when they are filling popcorn tubs. His meaning is obvious. He means that the fat lady is going to get even fatter tonight. He does not notice that she also reads his meaning. Perhaps he does not care.

Being a vampire is about waiting and watching. Nothing more romantic. There are no perks.

Think about it: to see in the dark, or hear the roaches seething behind the drywall, or smell in a crowded plaza exactly which women are menstruating, is nothing compared to the taste of a cold glass of cider on an autumn afternoon. Heightened senses does not mean improved senses. A bee can see in ultraviolet, but so what?

Look, do yourself a favor—bake a loaf of bread some spring morning. The real stuff. Smell the room as you work—the earthy, human quality. Feel the way the muscles in your arms bunch and relax as you knead the dough.

While the heat from baking warms the room, grind and prepare some coffee. Smell the fresh ground beans. Now tear yourself a piece of bread while the crust is still hot enough to hurt, butter it and devour.

What are the vampire's senses compared to this? Refocused. Dialed in on the hunt. Impatient for blood. And what is blood? Exotic perhaps. Sensuous at first. Ultimately, just food.

She takes her seat in the darkness of the theatre, a few rows away from the four other patrons. I am tempted to try taking her here. But I must be patient. If I attack too soon all I get is blood.

The movie starts. It's a good print.

I watch her watch the movie. Her mouth opens in tiny involuntary gasps of wonder at the people she watches on the screen. Her teeth are tiny and white, barely protruding from the gumline like baby's teeth.

I now have two hours in which I may do the only thing that satisfies me—dream.

I learned how to make love when I was thirteen. I had a paper route delivering to the Mar Vista Apartments, and once a month I had to go door-to-door bill collecting.

It was my favorite part of the job. I enjoyed seeing all the different people and peering past them into their little worlds. Hearing kids crying or *Star Trek* reruns or catching a whiff of hamburger and onions. Most of the people who came to the door were women, and I liked that. I especially liked seeing them casually, like sisters or aunts. Disheveled. In their element.

I liked one woman best. Mrs. Hackerel. Mrs. Hackerel was an ample woman, perhaps thirty-five years old. She wasn't fat, but rather had layers of insulating softness every-where, a form I was subsequently drawn to over and over again both during my life and afterwards. Her cheeks were round and pink. The muscles of her forearms hung down in a soft sort of way. It was a form of disguised strength, her arms. Soft but powerful, like a tiger hiding in a down pil-low. Mrs. Hackerel always appeared to be in the middle of baking a delicious blackberry pie, and I was completely in love with her.

Once a month I got to knock on her door and I learned to savor it. Mr. Hackerel was away in the Navy so I always knew she would answer. I depended upon it. Once Mrs. Hackerel came to the door in a housecoat, and while she was writing the check the lower folds parted and I caught a glimpse of soft white thigh and reddish brown hair. I had seen her secret, and what's more, I was pretty sure she knew it.

The reality of her body was beyond anything I had seen in the *Playboy* magazines I stole from the 7-Eleven after my route. Those women were arousing to me, but I felt that if I were to touch them their flesh would have the same slick texture as the centerfold. Mrs. Hackerel emanated warmth. She smelled like Diet Rite cola.

The glimpse I stole of her womanhood was a little secret we shared. I could see it in the way she smiled when she handed me her check each month. It was a little unspoken game we played, and both of us knew what the rules were. I had gotten a lucky glimpse and would always hope for more; she would guard her modesty, but admired my curiosity. Sometimes she would give me a cookie or a glass of lemonade, but it never went beyond that and never would.

Except, of course, one day it did.

I am standing at Mrs. Hackerel's door. The hallway smells like mildewed carpet. I ring the bell and wait. She is slow to respond. Finally, I hear her footsteps. I silently pray for the housecoat, or better, a sheer negligee like I have seen in *Playboy*. I want to see her breasts, her nipples. That thought literally makes me shiver. I want to see all of her creamy-smooth skin. But, of course, she wouldn't wear one of those. Not even if she knew I wanted her to. That thought nearly makes me sick with anxiety. That she should know how badly I want to see her body is my greatest fear and my greatest hope.

The chain rattles. The door opens. The woman who answers is not the woman I had expected. It is Mrs. Hackerel, but she is very different. She looks like she has been sleeping in the blue sun dress she is wearing. It is badly wrinkled and looks twisted somehow, like the sheets on my bed when I have been violently dreaming. She doesn't seem to notice. Her face looks puffy and red. Her hair, which is usually pulled back into a simple bun, spills down all around.

"Yes?" she says, very quietly. She doesn't seem to recognize me. For a mad moment I believe that she has forgotten how to bake, and that this accounts for her confusion and apparent sorrow.

"Collections, Mrs. Hackerel...for the *Times.*" Her eyes focus on me. Recognition flickers.

"Oh. Right. Come on in." She motions for me to follow. I notice the folded red, white and blue triangle sitting on the bureau. Mr. Hackerel's picture is missing.

The living room is dark, like a den. Candles float in glass bowls of water. Their light is the only light. It looks like a church. Mrs. Hackerel points me toward the kitchen to get some lemonade. This is wrong. She always gets it for me. But no, she is slumped into a chair at the dinette table, writing a check. I find the lemonade and pour it into a ceramic cup with Mr. Hackerel's ship's insignia on it, then I stand, as close as I dare, next to Mrs. Hackerel.

Finally, she looks up at me, sees the Navy cup, and begins to cry, because her husband has been killed at sea and isn't ever coming home.

I tried to be of comfort to her that day, but I was also being selfish. I wanted to touch her. I wanted to smell her hair, and she knew it. After a while she stopped crying, and looked up at me, into my eyes, and stared for a long time.

Then she took me by the hand, locked the door, led me to the room that she had shared with Mr. Hackerel, and proceeded to teach me.

My prey is fidgety. The movie is more than half over and in any case she already knows how it will end. The sensation is not enjoyable to her. She has planned her evening to perfection, but she is terribly aware of how she has decided to conclude things, and it is interfering with her ability to enjoy Cary Grant.

She shifts in her seat, too nervous even to enjoy her Red Vines. She checks her watch, sighs, and finally gives up on the film. She gets up and leaves, carefully throwing away the SuperSaver tub and the candy packaging on her way out. I follow, flickering in the shadows.

Blood is not a substitute for food or drink or sex. How could it be? Blood is merely the gateway which makes those other things possible. A vampire who has fed is human again.

For a while, anyway…

There are two vampires in the parking lot. My prey is bleeding from the soul and they smell it on the wind. The first swoops in before the theatre door has finished closing. Idiot. He isn't paying attention to her. She could still go either way. All he knows is his own hunger. He wants to live again. He wants to smell and touch and taste again. He probably kills five people for every one that nourishes him. He is reckless.

Just before he reaches her I step up from the shadows, grab him by the hair and yank him off his feet. While he is thrashing on the asphalt I tear his windpipe out.

All in silence and unseen.

My prey knows something is wrong but she hasn't figured out what. In any case she's the least of my worries. The lot is full of vampires.

Five, six…no, seven vampires are here, flowing on the wind like sheets of black silk. I cannot fight them and still have her. A mob of vampires is like a pack of hyenas. They obey no rules except their own bloodlust. All they know is that my prey is ripe and ready to eat.

Only she isn't really, not yet. She is following a plan and therein lies my chance.

She cannot see the vampires—they won't let her—but she can feel the danger. She is nervous already, which is good. I slide next to her and growl into her ear, "I'm gonna drink your blood for breakfast!" Then I let her see me, hungry, evil, right next to her.

It works. She doesn't want to die. Not like this. The others hesitate for a moment as she races to her car. I barely get inside with her and then we are off for home at sixty miles per hour.

Shaky, she fishes a single cigarette from her purse. Smoking is also part of the evening she has planned, but she is beginning to scramble the order of events.

Then she gets the giggles. Nervous giggles at first but I think she realizes that dying in the parking lot would not really have mattered much. She lowers her voice an octave and growls, "I'm gonna drink your blood for breakfast, buster!"

She's really pretty funny when she's by herself. Whimsy-funny, which is nice. Nice and sad.

I'm falling in love with my dinner. As usual.

Mrs. Hackerel was a patient teacher, but stern. She told me to undress, and then directed me as I undressed her. I was shaking so badly I could hardly unbutton her blouse, and her bra—well, she finally had to do that one herself.

She brought out a package of condoms and showed me how to use one. It was good that there were several of them. For the longest time, though, we didn't need them, for she insisted I go very slowly, exploring every part of her body, every vertebra, every follicle, each nail, slowly, with my eyes, my nose, my fingers, my lips, my tongue.

"It's about giving," she said. "It's about sharing. Take your time. Here is a place I like to be kissed. Here is a place I like to be touched..."

I got home very late that night and flustered through an excuse with my parents. By the next afternoon, Mrs. Hackerel had moved away.

My prey lives in a cramped apartment in Culver City. She has decorated it with old movie posters, particularly of Fred Astaire. Her home has been carefully cleaned and arranged in preparation for tonight. A selection of big band tunes awaits the touch of a button to fill the room. A cup with a bag of Twinings Earl Grey sits on the counter. Under a pillow on the bed, there is a vibrator with fresh batteries. In a drawer full of socks, there is a loaded gun. Finally, in one corner, sitting on a chair, is a life-sized, all-cotton replica of a man in top hat, tux and tails. My prey calls him "Mister Dobbin."

"Hello, Mister Dobbin," she says. "Are you ready? Oh, wonderful! Excuse me a moment, I have to go to the powder room." My prey goes to the bathroom and vomits. I envy her. I have wanted to throw up many times, when my belly was bursting with a dead man's blood and my mouth reeked with the taste of it, but my physiology doesn't work that way.

She cleans herself up, fixes her hair, and returns to the living room where Mister Dobbin awaits her. Taking him in her arms, she starts the music and dances with Mr. Dobbin to the sounds of Glen Miller.

Outside the window, I can hear vampires gathering.

How did I become a vampire? Simple. One night, one place, after a woman I loved had died, I became convinced that I wanted to die as well.

They found me and ate me. That's all. There's nothing more to say except this: if you're ever someplace and your instincts tell you something's wrong and to leave, even though your mind can see nothing to fear, listen to your instincts.

My prey sweeps round and round the room with Mr. Dobbin. She is giddy, manic, spinning ever faster. His floppy legs knock over a vase. She stumbles into the stereo and the CD restarts itself, but she doesn't stop. She is a centrifuge trying to separate out loneliness into its own black plasma that can be skimmed away and discarded.

She's making herself ugly. Desperate. Faster and faster. I hate this.

I trip her.

My prey falls into a heap with Mr. Dobbin, twisting her ankle. And a tiny miracle happens: when her face comes up from the floor I see something I've never seen in all the weeks of watching her. A flash of anger. She's scarlet with it. Her eyes dart the room like an angry child's, looking for her tormentor. She's been pushed before, I think, and I stand in awe, on a knife edge of emotion, because right now, ripe and fairly bursting with blood, *she is too dangerous to eat.*

She scans the room. I do not let her see me. *I'm afraid to.* She sees she is alone. "Idiot," she says. "You're a fat, clumsy idiot." And picks herself up.

My hunger returns.

My prey limps to the refrigerator for a piece of ice. She ices her ankle for a moment before she remembers that it will never have a chance to heal, and then angrily tosses the ice across the room. It smashes against the wall and shatters nicely, but she isn't watching. She hobbles over to where the gun is hidden and yanks it from the drawer. I see my opening.

"Please don't," I say, and let her see me. She gasps, recognizing me from the parking lot, and steps away. I'm presenting a nicer version now, though, and besides, like I said, nobody's ever surprised to see me. Not really.

"Why...why not?" she stammers.

"It'd be a waste. Last movie, last dance, why skip the last cup of tea?"

She stares me down, angrily. "What's the point? Last dinner, alone. Last movie, alone. Last dance..." she chokes on the word, "alone! Who needs to drink a stupid cup of tea all by herself!" Hot tears stream down her rosy cheeks. I want to go to her, comfort her. But of course I'm being selfish. I want to feel the warmth of her. I want to taste her blood.

"And over in the bed," I say, "under your pillow. The last...?" She stops crying instantly and glares at me, her face flushed with embarrassment. Flushed with blood.

"Get the hell out of here and leave me alone!"

"I'm here to drink your blood," I say, shrugging. She pales, the blood rushing to the center of her mass to protect itself, but she has her pride.

"Fine, go ahead, I'm gonna die tonight one way or another."

Suddenly I am furious. In two steps I wrap myself around her like a cloak and whisper into her ear.

"Lady you're already dead. As dead as I am. Your so-called life is a tissue of daydreams. So is mine. The difference is that I can't help it. You had a choice."

"That's not true!" She squirms in my arms, trying to get away. "You think it's easy to alone? To be...to be..."

"To be fat? To feel awkward? Do you know what I'd give to have what you have? To drink a cup of tea and taste it? To lie in bed and jerk off? To feel anything besides bloodlust? I've killed for that and will again. Soon." My face is pressed against her hair but I can't smell it. All I smell is blood.

Control, I need to regain control. She has to want this.

"Feel your heart racing," I say, "that's life." I kiss the back of her neck. My kiss is icy and her skin is instant gooseflesh. "When you shiver, that's life. The throbbing right now in your ankle means you are alive."

"No," she murmurs, "being held, even this way, *that* means I'm alive."

"No, you don't know..."

"I do know," she says, and turns in my arms to face me, places soft plump hands on either side of my face and pulls me towards her to kiss.

"I'm death," I tell her, "you don't want to kiss me."

"I'm alone," she replies, "and I'll kiss who I please."

We kiss, and ice meets fire. All the old lessons come back. Here is a place that's good to kiss. Here is a place that's nice to touch. I undress my prey slowly, the way that I have learned. She is soft. Her body is pink and has many rolls and folds.

I do the things I have learned to please her. But there is a limit. I cannot be aroused as a man. I will not let her even undress me. The coldness of my caresses will soon lose their novelty and she will grow afraid. Her skin is flushed with warmth and life. I am very hungry. I trace my finger lightly around her breasts and down her warm belly. She shivers and moans in my arms. Here is a place to touch. I caress her there and when I am sure she is distracted, I sink my teeth into the artery in her neck. Her blood is rich with the flavors of the evening, cheap Chardonnay, buttered popcorn, Red Vines, hormones. She is on the verge of climax, but the blood loss will deny her even that. Now she can feel what is happening. She is afraid now. She tries feebly to push me away, but this does her no good. I am so hungry and the blood tastes so good I am drawing the life out of her with all my strength. I feel like I am sucking from the bottom of my feet I draw so hard. I can feel the life draining out of her and into me. I can feel myself almost alive again. I can smell her hair now. I can smell her sweat, bittersweet with her sex. I am warm again. I am alive again.

And I am killing her. She grows heavy in my arms. She whimpers. I am so hungry and she tastes so good but she is dying and I love her and it's about giving.

Giving.... I stop. She is on the verge of death. One foot in the grave. I lay her down on the bed. I am still hungry. I need to finish. But there is something I can give.

"This is death," I say. "This coldness. This emptiness. This is what you chose." Her eyes flicker, I can see the whites. She is afraid.

That's the easy part. I can give her something genuine (but I want her life in me!). I breathe deeply (I can smell the ice melting!), close my eyes, force the words: "You can die or you can live..." She stares at me, mute. Another deep breath, "if you fight me...you can win."

Done. She has heard me.

I attack.

Her arms come up to fend me off but they are easy to push aside. Her neck is bloody. The wounds spurt with her panicky heart. My jaw distends, hungry—

And she grabs my hair. Yanks my hair in two fat fistfuls. Twists my aim just enough so that my skull rams into the headboard.

Rage! I am all rage and hunger. She is rolling away and I am clawing at her fat back and her bloody skin is under my nails and it is maddening. I want her life in me! She throws a pillow and I rip it into pieces. Feathers and blood. She throws something harmless—that idiot vibrator. I throw it back and hit her head but she is still moving away. She is faster than I thought. She wants to live more than I thought. Why why why did I ever stop drinking! She's pulling, yanking at a drawer and now she has a—

Gun.

We pause, heaving. She is grey, bloody, naked. Absurd in her obesity. Leaning against a door frame. Feathers drifting in the air making my eyes itch (allergies! how long since I felt...).

"You cannot kill me," I say.

"Perhaps," she wheezes, "but I bet I can make holes in you. I bet I can make everything you took from me come pouring back out."

Oh god oh god oh god no.... I shift my weight, the gun follows. I take a step forward. She draws back the hammer.

Click.

"Please..." Oh god I'm begging...

"You gave me a chance just now, and I think that was hard for you." Pause. Wheeze. "I am afraid...and I just want to shoot you. This is hard. You go now."

"Please, just a..."

"Go now!" She isn't loud but she means it.

Outside her apartment the vampires are dispersing. They can smell the change in the wind. She has decided and they cannot finish her. They cannot harm me either. I am only half filled, but that gives me power. They float away like black autumn leaves.

The sky is glowing a pre-dawn purple. I am weak and unsatisfied. My human senses are already fading. Fear of the light drives me back to the grave.

There is a bakery that I often pass on my way and this morning I pause to watch the men work—mixing dough in industrial mixers, shaping loaves in pans. They work efficiently and I feel humbled.

I am a carrion bird and not a very good one. I am weak and sentimental and I am too often hungry.

And yet...if you could have seen her when she faced me down: fierce and ridiculous all in one moment—a flabby gunslinger—gloriously alive...

The wind shifts and a buttery, yeasty whiff of the day's bread baking broadsides my fading senses.

I love her. I am proud of her.

...And for one crystalline moment, I feel a pang of honest, human, hunger in my gut.

Benjamin Gorman

Lament

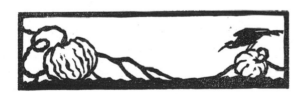

from
1992
"Lament" is the first of three poems in this volume by Ben Gorman, who, besides being a talented graphic artist (he designed and typeset this book) is also dedicated to the sonnet.

I won't introduce each poem individually, because it wouldn't do to have the introductions use more words than the poems themselves. Suffice to say that Ben can say a lot with a little and that, during a long night of stories, it was always a delight to see him get up to read with a single sheet of paper in his hands!

Lament

by Benjamin Gorman

Through drapeless windows facing Autumn's grey
A dusky light invades my empty room,
But fails to banish shadows thick as clay
Or lift the stony silence of the tomb.

For occupants, a desk and chair remain,
Where I would pen my verses strong and proud;
Where once my writings masked the wooden grain,
A layer of dust has settled like a shroud.

No longer can I enter now to write,
Though by my soul I long for nothing more;
My fate affords me no more rare delight
Than this pale glimpse of all my life before.

On Autumn's winds now blow my dreams of fame,
For since my death things haven't been the same.

Steven V. Taylor

Scooter Tillis and the Bag of Nutritious Snacks

from

_1995_

If you're going to invite a bunch of people to write Halloween tales and come to your house to read them, you're going to hear a lot of trick-or-treat stories. It's only natural. People draw from their own experience when they write, and almost everybody associates Halloween with trick-or-treating.

Over the course of ten years, we heard lots of trick-or-treat stories of all stripes—from reminiscences, to comic adventures to disturbingly real stories about the dangers of kids alone on the street—but none were as evocative or as funny as Steve Taylor's "Scooter Tillis and the Bag of Nutritious Snacks."

Steve's substantial energies are spent as lead guitarist, vocalist and songwriter for The Uninvited, a very popular West Coast band which this year released their first album for Atlantic/Igloo Records. Before that, he held down jobs ranging from third mate on a freighter supplying oil rigs in the Bering Sea to writing copy for a radio show entitled "This Week In Rock & Roll."

Steve has always had a very wry writing style, and whenever he got up to read, people knew they were going to laugh. This story is his favorite of his contributions, and it's ours as well.

Scooter Tillis and the Bag of Nutritious Snacks

by Steven V. Taylor

Halloween, 1954

At 107 miles per hour, the tires barely stuck to the road as the old Buick station wagon careened down the empty highway that ran along Lake Wolford. With one hand on the wheel and the other on his 13th Hershey Bar, nine-year-old Hop-along Scooter Tillis, the Trick-or-Treat King, was bringing in his greatest haul ever: no fewer than seven gunnysacks stuffed with Halloween goodies were packed tightly into the back of the wagon.

Of course, if his parents ever found out he stole the car to broaden his trick-or-treating radius this would also be his last Halloween. But Hop-along wasn't worried. He could still make the next ten miles in seven minutes, which meant he would be home in bed before his parents got back from their Halloween party, and no one would suspect a thing. With a grin of satisfaction, he put the pedal down.

Unfortunately, Detroit never took into consideration pilfering nine-year-olds when they designed this particular station wagon, and Scooter was having a problem seeing over the dashboard. Thus, he didn't see the deer that stepped into the road that night. In fact, he had absolutely no idea what went wrong when the car flipped end over end, rolled seven times, and finally hit the lake where it sank to the bottom in a matter of seconds...

25

Two weeks later, the local authorities found the old Buick and dragged it out of the lake. Inside, there was no trace of Scooter Tillis, and no body was ever found. The police did recover, however, all seven gunnysacks full of wet candy, and the news of the greatest feat of trick-or-treating in history spread among kids throughout the county. Granted, Scooter Tillis had previously established himself as the Trick-or-Treat King, but seven gunnysacks! That was the stuff of legend...

Halloween, 1995

The fate of this year's candy haul hung in the balance. Mrs. Rickenbacker stood before her two sons holding a trick-or-treat bag in each hand. The one on the right was cool. It was covered with laughing skulls on a black background, but more importantly, it always produced an excellent yield. The one on the left, however, was known between the brothers as The Bag of Nutritious Snacks. Somehow, the damn thing was cursed. No matter what neighborhood, no matter what house, no matter what generous widow you might visit, if you were holding the BONS—short for Bag of Nutritious Snacks—you were going to get an apple. It was almost scary. You could be standing in a doorway with ten other trick-or-treaters while some kind old man doled out king-size Abazabas and Snickers, but when he finally gets to you and the BONS, he runs out. Invariably, the old man's statement, "Wait right here, young man, I'll see if I can find something..." is followed by the horrible sound of an apple hitting the bottom of your bag.

Scotty was an authority on this phenomenon. For the last three Halloweens he had been the BONS's unfortunate toter—not by choice, of course. Scotty was always yielding to the insistent fists of his older brother, Brian, who didn't want the bag to tarnish his reputation as the greatest trick-or-treater on the block. Brian also took a perverse pleasure in his little brother's trick-or-treating misfortune. At the conclusion of last Halloween, as Scotty walked miserably through the door dragging a bag full of apples, Brian heralded his little brother's arrival: "Ladies and Gentlemen, just in from Washington State, it's Mr. Golden Delicious!"

But that was last year, and now the success or failure of this Halloween was about to be determined. The brothers stood there, transfixed by the two bags clutched in their mother's hands. Finally, the moment of truth: "Okay," Mrs. Rickenbacker said, "I think that Brian had the skull bag last time, so Scotty gets it this time."

A wave of Halloween bliss washed over Scotty as he took the bag from his mother's hand. The faint scent of last year's Junior Mints was still perceptible in the bag, and Scotty breathed deeply of the heavenly fragrance. This Halloween was not going to suck. He could already hear the rattle of the M&M's as the mini-packets fell into his bag by the handful…

A searing bolt of pain knocked Scotty from his trick or treating reverie. It might have been a fist or it could have been a boot—most likely it was a combination of both. The only thing Scotty knew at that moment was that something hit him hard, and now he was writhing on the floor in pain with the Bag of Nutritious Snacks pulled over his head.

Freeing himself from the bag, the scenario became clear. The second his mother had left the room, Brian sucker-punched him and took the cool bag. Scotty knew better. He should have clung to his mother's calf the moment she'd handed it to him—he was just too caught up in the rapture of actually holding the thing. Brian turned to him just before he left the room with the cool bag. "Give my regards to Granny Smith!" he laughed.

Of course, there was no sense in telling mom. That would only result in a boundless cornucopia of terror. Best to just put on the costume and get this whole thing over with.

Fifteen minutes later he was walking out into the cool Halloween evening with Brian. Scotty was dressed as a Mutant Ninja Turtle, while Brian, who was 14, was the same thing he was last year—a drive-by shooting victim. The costume was simple yet effective: blue jeans and a tee shirt with holes in it, each one dripping a copious amount of blood.

"Now you watch over your little brother, Brian," Mrs. Rickenbacker said as she closed the door behind them, totally oblivious to the earlier bag-switch.

After hitting the fifth house, Brian split. Actually, Scotty was surprised he hung out that long. Last year, the front door was barely closed before Brian ditched him to go terrorize the neighborhood with his friends.

As for the Bag of Nutritious Snacks, the curse was still in full effect. In seven houses he garnered five apples, one banana and a granola bar. He figured at this rate he should be able to open a health food store by the end of the night. House after house, block after block, the strange bag worked its twisted magic. Finally, Scotty had had enough. Dragging his pathetic bag behind him, he set his sights for next Halloween and started walking miserably back home even though he had two hours left before his curfew.

The boy was so depressed over his situation, he didn't even notice the station wagon that had pulled up next to him. Lost in his despair, he had no idea the car was cruising along, matching his painfully slow pace, until he heard a voice. "Alright, Bucko, gimme the bag!"

Startled, Scotty finally noticed the vehicle. The passenger side window was rolled down, but there was no passenger on the bench seat. The driver, concealed in the darkness, was pointing a cap gun. The toy was an old-fashioned number—chrome-plated with a plastic handle, about one-quarter the size of a real Colt .45. A short tongue of spent red caps curled off the top. "You heard me!" said the young voice. "Toss the bag in the car!"

Scotty couldn't believe it. He was being held up by a guy with a cap gun. Fine. He had nothing to lose. In fact, it was a good chance to be rid of the Bag of Nutritious Snacks forever. Without saying a word, he dropped the bag in the passenger window and continued down the street.

The car, however, still rolled slowly along beside him. Inside, Scotty could hear the thief shuffling through his booty, and was unsurprised when he heard the voice again. "Hey, Carmen Miranda—what's with the fruit?"

"Leave me alone," was Scotty's only reply. The station wagon, however, continued to roll along beside the boy for several more yards until the driver spoke again.

"Look kid, can I talk to you?"

Against his better judgment, Scotty stopped and looked into the car. Behind the wheel sat a young boy no older than himself. He wore an old-fashioned cowboy outfit complete with plastic chaps, cap guns and a vinyl cowboy vest. Around his neck he wore a huge bandanna that hung all the way to his waist, and the whole get-up was topped with a wide-brimmed Pony Express-style cowboy hat that was about five sizes too big.

"Look, I'm alone tonight, and looks like you need a little help," said the driver. "Why don't you come with me and we can work this town together." Scotty felt a certain trepidation. This kid was obviously way too young to drive and besides, he had just tried to rob him. On the other hand, this Halloween was quickly turning into the suckiest event of his childhood and 15 years from now it might cost him thousands of dollars in psychotherapy. Best to take a chance and hopefully turn this thing around. With a shrug of his shoulders, Scotty jumped into the car.

"I'm Scotty Rickenbacker," he said as they pulled away from the curb.

"I'm Hop-along Scooter Tillis, the Trick-or-Treat King," said the boy behind the wheel. Scotty thought that was a pretty cool thing to dress up as. Everyone knew the story of Scooter Tillis and how he died with all those Halloween treats in his car. But most kids had stopped dressing up as Hop-along because being a cowboy was, well, geeky.

The two kids rode along in silence until Scooter pulled into a 7-Eleven. "Our first stop," he said to Scotty while getting out of the car. Scotty was baffled. A 7-Eleven? Who goes trick-or-treating at a 7-Eleven? As they walked into the store, Scooter pulled his bandanna up over his nose and drew his cap gun. The bored teenager at the cash register didn't even look up from his *Playboy* when the duo stepped up to the counter. Scooter pulled a gunnysack out of nowhere and threw it at him. "Fill it up with candy and don't skimp on the Hershey Bars!" he exclaimed.

The teenager was clearly pissed to be interrupted by this brazen little brat. "What's this?" he yelled. "Get the hell outta here before I beat the crap outta both of ya!"

Scooter shifted the aim of his cap gun one foot to the right of the young man behind the counter. Suddenly, the gun went off with a report louder than any magnum Dirty Harry ever used. The coffee pot on the other side of the store exploded into a fountain of decaf and glass shards. Shifting another inch to the left, Scooter blew out a glass door on the refrigerated drink racks, followed by six bottles of Snapple. Shifting his aim back to the teenager, he restated his demands. "Now let's get on with it!"

Amazed, confused and plainly terrified, the teenager started frantically stuffing the sack with both hands. As he hurried about his task, Scooter offered guidance. "More Snickers...no Gummy Bears...yeah, we'll take the Kit-Kats...Christ, doesn't this joint have any Good 'n' Plenty?"

Moments later, Scooter heaved the overstuffed bag over his shoulder and walked determinedly for the door. "Come on, Scott, let's skidoo before the sheriff comes." Scotty, mouth agape, could only do as Scooter suggested. Car doors slamming, the two pint-sized *banditos* sped out of the parking lot.

All Scotty could do was stare out the windshield in shock. He'd seen everything with his own eyes...and those weren't like any cap guns he'd seen before. Slowly, the reality of the last ten minutes began to sink in. "I just robbed a 7-Eleven," he said out loud. At nine years old, Scotty usually relied on his mother to clear up any ethical ambiguities. 'Is it okay, Mom?' he would ask before doing just about anything. But armed robbery—he didn't need his mom to tell him that *that* definitely fell on the naughty side of Santa's list. In his mind's eye he could see ol' St. Nick stuffing Scotty's stocking so full of coal he could heat the neighborhood for a week.

Yes, a cowardly retreat followed immediately by a groveling, tear-stained confession seemed like the best plan of action. Keeping a discrete eye on Scooter, Scotty slowly reached for the car door handle with one hand and his bag with the other. The Bag of Nutritious Snacks. Scotty noticed that somehow all the fruit roll-ups from the 7-Eleven heist had ended up in the BONS. It was too much. Suddenly, Christmas, Santa Claus and his mother were a million years away, and Halloween was right now. *Forget it,* he thought to himself, *I'm going to ride with Scooter Tillis, or whoever he is, and at the end of tonight, I'm going to eat something that's bad for my teeth.*

The two kids tore up the town. At every house they visited, if a bowl was brought out, Scotty's partner found a way to discretely empty it. If they were in a crowd of trick-or-treaters, Hop-along would quietly cut out the bottom of everyone's bag with his tiny pocket knife, collecting the precious booty from the unsuspecting vampires, witches, and Spidermen. Pound after pound of candy was stuffed into the gunnysacks Scooter amassed in the back of his station wagon. Soon the back of the car had turned into some kind of twisted dental nightmare, with enough sugar to throw Scotty's entire elementary school population into pancreatic convulsions. It was wonderful. It was amazing. Of course, not every encounter went smoothly, and a hasty retreat was called for on several occasions, complete with screeching tires, triumphant hollering, and Scooter firing off his howitzer-cap gun-from-hell as they sped into the night.

Finally, at exactly five minutes before Scotty's curfew, the old station wagon pulled up in front of Scotty's house. Scooter slipped the behemoth into park, looked over at his partner, and drew his cap gun, or whatever it was. "Well," he said as he waved the pistol nonchalantly, "this is where our trails part. I guess you knew I was going to keep all the candy…"

"What?!" exclaimed Scotty.

"…Yeah," Scooter Tillis continued, "but you can keep the bag of produce; I'm not much into roughage. Well, tell ya what. Here's a king-size Baby Ruth. Gotta go!" Instantly, Scotty was inexplicably ejected from the vehicle by a force that left him sprawled on the lawn amidst scattered healthy snacks from the BONS. As his composure returned he could hear the sound of the old station wagon fading in the distance, punctuated by the barely discernible report of Scooter's cap gun.

He looked down at the Baby Ruth he still clutched in his hand—the only remnant of his strange adventure—but his thoughts were interrupted by the sound of his older brother's voice. "Nice candy bar—it's mine." And with that, Brian snatched away the evening's meager haul.

Scotty snapped. He rose to his feet to pummel his brother's knuckles with the soft, fleshy parts of his body, but before the violence could begin they were both distracted by the sound of a prepubescent mob raging angrily up the street.

Scotty had counted as high as 42 pissed-off trick-or-treaters when someone in the gathering yelled, "Hey! That's *him!* That's one of the guys who stole our candy!" A collective wail rose from the mob as it surged like a wave toward the brothers. Scotty instinctively turned to run for the safety of his house, but Brian—who had no idea what the crowd was yelling about but was happy to know it would cause his brother pain and anguish—grabbed Scotty by the shell of his Ninja turtle costume and screamed, "Here he is! Come and get him!"

Scotty did his best to assume the fetal position in hopes of prolonging his life an extra few seconds. Then out of nowhere came the sound of a station wagon engaged in a four-wheel power-slide. The prehistoric Buick came to a dramatic rest about six inches from the edge of the mob, and out jumped a small boy in an oversized cowboy outfit. Before the words "Who the hell are you?" could leave Brian's lips he was hanging by his ankle from a limb of the big oak tree outside the Rickenbacker's house. No one saw how it happened. A quick *whoosh* sound, and there was Brian, dangling upside-down by a jump rope.

Scooter turned and addressed the stunned crowd. "That guy has all your stuff...kinda looks like a piñata, don't he?" As Hop-along turned back towards his trusty station wagon, the ugly mob advanced on Brian with their plastic pirate swords, their small red pitchforks, and other pain-inducing costume accessories. Scotty, however, didn't get a chance to say anything before Scooter and the station wagon completely disappeared.

Pausing for a moment to listen to Brian's screams, Scotty started into the house when he noticed his brother's bulging sack of goodies resting by the front door. He picked it up and walked inside, leaving the Bag of Nutritious Snacks in its place.

Edith Weil

The India
Rubber Foot
Factory

from
1994

When Edith Weil got up to read in 1994, it was immediately clear that she had something special. To begin with, she wasn't carrying the usual handful of pages. She was carrying a laptop computer. She asked us to turn off the lights, and when we did, she read directly from the screen, her face bathed in an eerie blue glow.

The arrival of a computer that night heralded an interesting storytelling theme that we would see repeated in various forms—the clash of the primarily rural Halloween tradition (it's a harvest festival, after all) with the look and feel and sound of the urban environment.

Edith arrived in Los Angeles in 1985 to attend USC film school and gradually worked her way into a position as an editor on such television shows as "Brooklyn South" and "NYPD Blue." She's had a lot of time over the years to watch how the Hollywood game is played, and to ruminate on the strange combination of luck, ambition and charisma that elevates some people above others in our collective eyes, and makes them famous. This observation informs her writing generally, and this story in particular.

Because, despite what the title implies, this is a Hollywood story.

The India Rubber Foot Factory

by Edith Weil

"Have you ever heard the sound of rubber feet on a marble floor?" I shook my pleasantly sotted head feebly, starting to reply. "It is the most God-awful screech..." the Legionnaire said, firmly clasping his highball glass.

We were in a bar on Hollywood Boulevard, and it was Halloween night. My face was paled with white semi-translucent makeup, my hair hanging around my shoulders in lustrous locks, dyed unnaturally black. Lips white, eyes sunken, clothes tattered, hanging in a sultry fashion off my shoulder. I was an Undead Creature of the Night. My bladder was full, but so was my glass, and I would not risk my seat simply to banish the urine from my gut. Who stalked the earth? The Undead. Did the Undead need to attend to bodily functions? Certainly not. And neither would I.

The gathering crowd darkened the doorway, waiting impatiently for a space to open up, taxing the bouncers' goodwill. The tiny room already sustained end-to-end tides of inbound and outbound revelers, swaying to and fro in an infinite trek from the tiny bathroom in the back to the clogged front entrance. Grease-painted girl-kittens, Conan the Barbarians, Vampiras, Elviras and Leisure Suit Larrys slowly squeezed their sweaty flesh intimately past one another, grease on grease, sequin on sequin. The air exploded with loud unclever remarks.

Opposite the bar, in their own sparsely populated world of cafe tables, elegant pillars and hanging plants, were the

39

great embellished remains of many a deceased movie star. Humphrey Bogart, Katharine Hepburn, Bette Davis and countless others, stuck in time, their fingers curling backwards in elegant brush strokes, chins jutted out, teeth clenched, permanently gray in their swirling skirts and natty sports jackets on the yellowing paper.

An hour earlier the seat beside mine became free. That's when the Legionnaire sat down. His doughy face hung in folds about his mouth, looking ready to drip to the ground. He had steady, serious eyes, yet as he talked, the folds of his jowls moved all on their own, owing nothing to what a face should be doing. When he smiled, his eyes and lips looked like cherries and raisins drowning in whipped cream. Still, it was a nice face. I liked it. A face I wanted to know better. He lit up awkwardly as he told a story, and he didn't know what to do with his hands. So unlike most of the people in this city, this bar. So sure, they were. So sure that they, above all others, would end up one of the Famous. Someday immortalized on that wall—or one just like it— recorded in history as a recognizable caricature. But I was different. I had a plan.

What is truly holy about movies is that they are a conduit to intimacy—intimacy with the image, with the hero, but mostly with yourself. Study a face, a gesture, a wince, a smile, in great detail, and decide if you aren't really studying the perfection to which you aspire. And if you are one of the Players—well, you are a minister of affirmation of the glory of humanity. You are a shaman, a holy leader. You transport the human condition to angels' wings. Stardom is pre-ordained from the heavens. In the annals of the history of All There Is, is written: "this person shall be famous and this person shall not" in monarch letters on an invisible ledger. My name was there. I knew it. It was a matter of finding the key to unlock the lock.

"Haven't seen a crowd like this since India," the Legionnaire pronounced loudly, steadying his drink to his lips.

"Yeah, Halloween's a killer," I shouted above the din. Did he say India? A Legionnaire. India. This guy played his part. Took the Halloween tradition seriously. And I liked that.

"It wasn't on Halloween, though, that crowd," he continued. "No, it was the occasion of the arrival of the town surgeon. In India."

He then ceased talking and drank well, letting his face settle back to its doughy state, absorbed in some affectation of memory.

"When I was in the service," the Legionnaire eventually continued, "I heard of a town where rubber feet were manufactured for amputees." His cheeks jumped up to just under his eyes. "India, you know, has rubber out the blowhole, you might say—pardon my coarseness. Far more available than plastic or wood for prosthetics, and just as effective—or effective enough, if I am to understand correctly."

"Oh yes, there's a lot of rubber in India," I said dociley, then went on about the rubber industry: chewing gum, truck tires, plantations and politics. A hoax was a hoax. If he had been to India, I could certainly be an expert on rubber. The Legionnaire listened and drank, smiling every now and again. Then he spoke up.

"Some manufacturers have done very well. Very well indeed. So well, in fact, that the owners and even the workers of the plants have had their real feet removed and replaced with rubber substitutes. Why, yes, I've heard in some parts it's become quite the thing."

Quite the thing. The image of it reeled. What a story this one was concocting. I liked him all the more for it.

"Whole towns, in fact. All chopping off their limbs."
My friend gestured with blustery animation as he worked
up his tale. "Lining up to do it, too. On some mornings the
din of chirping and squeaking made by feet upon pavement
made it seem that the entire town was blessed with prosperity. They were rolling in it. Old women hobbled around
happily, jugs on their heads and smiles on their faces. Yes, it
took time to get the balance just so, so one's clay pot
wouldn't come crashing down, but everyone learned after a
fashion. And of course the children all got the hang of it
immediately.

"Ended up, I was stationed in this very town when I
was on active duty. At first I couldn't believe what I was seeing. Practically the whole town—except, of course, for the
very young and the very old.... Well, needless to say, I got
to know one of the factory owners fairly well. And he
seemed pleased. Good for business. 'Prosperity,' he said,
'demanded sacrifice and gratitude. How would it look for a
manufacturer not to stand behind his own product, so to
speak? After all, they're just as good as real feet,' he said,
and squeaked away across the marble floor of his mansion.

"It came to be believed that the rubber feet had special
curative powers, and over time the sick and destitute
crowded the town—hoping to obtain rubber feet to cure
their poverty and disease. Sure, it was easy enough to have
your feet removed. The sad part about it was most of them
had no money to buy rubber feet to replace the real ones.
The population of beggars increased—footless and dirty,
crying over their fresh amputations, insisting that rubber
feet be given over. Now. For free. They would have made a
run on the factory if they could, but alas, they could not."

"Quite a story," I offered as the Legionnaire climbed
down from his reverie. "Must have taken you a week to

concoct it. Are you an actor? Or a writer? I mean, it's really, really good."

The Legionnaire blinked. His face had settled down to its unmoving state, weighty and placid. "It's true," he said, mildly alarmed, mildly defensive. "You don't believe me." He slammed his glass on the bar, some of the drink sloshing over the side. Turning fully to face me he said, "You don't believe me? Fine. Don't. I don't believe you either. You're not a...a whatever you are. You're just some person working a day job, waiting tables or serving drinks. Am I right? Table-waiting? Drink-getting? 'What can I get you this evening, sir? Would you like an olive in your martini? I'm sorry your steak is overdone. May I bring you another?' Living on tips and kind words. I'll bet you think your big break is just around the corner. That you'd never be so foolish as to amputate your own feet to replace them with healing rubber ones." His eyes had become hard and round with intensity. Then he settled back to his drink, sullen and disdainful.

I gathered my things about me. "You think you know who I am," I ventured, from my lair of hurt pride. "Think you're so clever, so right about me. Well, I don't wait tables and I don't serve drinks, Mr. Fantastic Story. You want to know what I do? I'll tell you what. You come around to Warner Brothers, and you'll see what I do..." But I was cut off in my retort—because at that moment he looked up at me, his eyes now sad, lustrous, like brown velvet, his face hung in a hurt expression, and I blurted out, "Let's get a hotel."

Movies are an offering from Star to Viewer. Here, it says, examine me. Fall in love with me. Know me in my largest moments and my most small—better than you know yourself. Is the hero's life any less valid than your own? His personality any less opaque than yours? No. In fact, these characters are more real than you or your life because you imbue them with your image. They are your *doppelgangers*, but they do the things that you cannot.

It was 3:10, to be exact. I popped open my eyes briefly to catch a glimpse of the VCR blinking steadily. The room was dark except for a yellow light seeping in around the window shade. I turned on my side, anticipating a small question in my gut, empty now, yet giddy. I reached over tentatively to see if the Legionnaire was still in the bed— and had my answer. The bed was empty. Crushing hurt and joyous relief flooded me briefly, as my scalp tingled with anxiety. Okay, good, that was over.

Then, from beyond the hallway partition, a light went on. The bathroom light. Joy and anxiety cruised though my nervous system once again, tightening my solar plexus— but I pushed them down. What was I doing with this jowly mystery man? I closed my eyes, willing the thoughts to recede and sleep to come on. Bats and bonfires, demons and witches floated upward in dreamlike scenario. He climbed back into the hotel bed we shared, friends and strangers both, when suddenly the question that had been forming in my sleepy brain crystallized. My eyes shot open: "Was that squeaking I just heard...?"

It's been three months now and I've gotten the hang of walking, even dancing. I have to say my luck's improved. I've had five auditions in the last two weeks. Two of them were callbacks. The Legionnaire moved in with me and we performed the operation in my apartment. It wasn't so bad, not when you have the proper tools. The feet—well, they're not exactly my flesh color, so I can't wear clear panty hose.

But I've been able to wear size 8 shoes for the first time in my life. When I get a little money I'm going to get special custom ones to match my skin color. Producers look at feet, you know. Let me tell you.

Ed W. Marsh

Dark Vegas

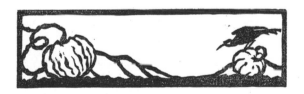

from 1991

Nineteen ninety-one was an excellent year for spook stories. Three of the stories in this book, more than from any other year, were written and read in 1991.

Ed Marsh is a filmmaker who has held the usual creative person's cornucopia of jobs, including editing the "director's cut" of James Cameron's The Abyss, and, more recently, writing and producing the HBO Special, The Making of Titanic, as well as writing the bestselling book on the same subject, James Cameron's Titanic.

Ed was a sporadic guest at our parties, but when he came, he always brought something thought-provoking and quietly creepy. He explains the origin of "Dark Vegas" this way:

> I was working on an action movie at Hoover Dam. We basically had the run of the place so it was hard to resist exploring. I'll never forget entering the staircase with no beginning and no end. Down there in the darkness, cement on all sides of us, it felt as if we'd found the secret entrance to Hell itself. Combine that with a few evenings spent in Las Vegas, and the mental connections which became "Dark Vegas" aren't hard to imagine.

Dark Vegas

by Ed W. Marsh

*He knew the city itself was not inherently evil. On the contrary,
the city held evil captive—trapped it in a neon prison...*

Samuel Taylor had just finished a lucrative assignment
customizing a vast network of lab tubing for CalTech when
a friend had invited him out to the desert to take a break
and to meet the old man.

Jerry was eighty-five, and to hear him talk he had
shaped every thousand-watt tube from Vegas to Reno.
"Hilton Flamingo? All that pink? My idea!" he shouted
over the screech of the focused baby-blue flame. "Never
saw a nickel for it." His skin had that unnatural burnt-
orange tan one gets from working hot glass. Only his
crow's feet were white, as if tiny spiders had woven intricate
webs to protect each black pearl eye.

Yet, while the man had darkened in the constant presence of the strong ultraviolet, his possessions had faded: a
photo frame on the workbench displayed a family of faceless ghosts; color snapshots of various casinos Jerry had lit
looked more like X-rays of strange creatures from another
planet; and the brittle documents taped to the cinder block
walls with yellowed and cracking masking tape looked more
like the Dead Sea Scrolls than any sort of certificates or
diplomas. It was only after eye-straining scrutiny that
Samuel found out one of them was a history doctorate from
Yale, dated 1928. Old Jerry was a PhD. "...And a regular
S.O.B. Now I'm just O.L.D. and a card-carrying member

of A.A.R.P.! Fat lot of good that degree did me during the depression," he laughed. He'd come to Nevada to study the vanishing Indian cultures but at the last minute lost his grant and ended up working the maws of the hellish casting furnaces slowly giving birth to Hoover Dam's metal spine. Addicted to the flame, he'd next turned his talents to the burgeoning neon business.

Samuel watched reverently as Jerry hefted an opaque twenty-footer from the rack and positioned it over the fire. The largest tube Samuel had ever worked was shorter than his outstretched arms and thinner than a pencil. As the tube caught the glow Jerry began a casual movement around the flame, sliding the tube back and forth in his ungloved hand, letting gravity pull pattern into the once-straight line. The cackling old man was silent at his work, fully focused on the flame and the glass. Never once did he refer to the client specs which sat, forgotten (supposedly memorized), beneath a week's worth of beer cans.

Was it Moses who had turned staffs into serpents? Samuel couldn't remember for sure, but that's what the work reminded him of. An effortless magic act, a shaman working the holy fire. Within minutes, Jerry had turned the massive hollow rod into a flawless rose. Pumped full of argon, the flower was destined to shine its delicate blue petals in the new wing of the Tropicana.

Samuel was hooked. In less than three weeks he had finished his freelance assignments back in California and rented a small apartment in nearby Henderson. Jerry warned him that he wasn't really looking for help, but Samuel was persistent. He hung out at the workshop, watching the old man dance the glass over the flame, buying him the occasional beer and listening to his stories which came few and far between and never while working the glass. Oftentimes, Jerry would stop a story mid-sentence after picking up a tube and then continue it from that very point half an hour later after bedding the twisted tube in the cooling locker.

Two weeks into it, Jerry landed a rush contract for the Desert Inn. Even then he was reluctant to let Samuel work the flame. "This ain't like your puny lab tubing, son. This takes patience of the chess-playing variety. The weight of these rods makes 'em want to explode before they'll bend, unless you heat 'em just right." But after Samuel had proved his worth by putting a square-knot in a ten-footer (without pinching the hollow) he began his apprenticeship under Jerry in earnest and they completed the contract with two days to spare.

To avoid the stifling desert heat, they worked mostly at night, throwing the warehouse doors wide open. The small, potent flames would throw their shadows dancing across the sands, reaching towards the more distant fire that was the city at night.

They almost never talked when they worked, so it took a while for Samuel to form his private opinion that Jerry was just a little bit crazy. One night Samuel was twisting some replacements for Caesar's—long green tubes that would be laid out end to end around the building. They were a cinch to make, requiring little more than measuring and sizing, but Jerry kept asking for extra twists that messed up his lengths and wouldn't even show once the tubes were mounted. He asked Jerry why.

"See there?" The old man gestured to a small knot of glass, still glowing a dull yellow. "Sanskrit. Spells *ka* which means 'soul.' It's part of a prayer I put up on Caesar's Palace. If you don't put the words into those replacements then the prayer won't be any good."

"You serious? You can't even see it," complained Samuel.

"Don't have to." With that, Jerry had resumed work on his own project, reluctant to say more. Samuel had complied, more than a little miffed at what he considered a pointless complication. As the night wore on, however, he found that he couldn't concentrate. In all, there seemed to be twelve distinct words repeated over and over as the prayer wrapped itself around Caesar's. He was so distracted that he cracked three twenty-footers in a row.

The next night, when Samuel arrived at work, the flames were off. Jerry was leaning against his jeep. "Way you were burning through the tubes last night'll put us out of business. Can't afford to keep you curious." Samuel smiled. "Hop in," he said, "we're goin' on a field trip."

They were on a dirt road headed for Boulder City. The moonlight was strong enough for Jerry to drive without headlights, a ritual he obviously enjoyed. The open jeep was freezing. Samuel wrapped an old painter's tarp around himself for warmth.

"Desert tends to polarize things," said Jerry. "Hot, cold, water, sand. Even Good and Evil." He took a long drag on his cigarette. The red-hot tip mimicked poorly the hundreds of stars in the sky around them. "Ever hear of a place called Sedona?"

"Arizona, right? One of those hippy places where the New Age people go to charge their crystals?"

"They almost got it right. Indians known it practically forever. Whole place just emanates warmth and goodness. I'd like to retire there if I can afford it." The old man was silent for a minute as he slowed his jeep over a long-neglected cattle crossing. "Guess I don't have to tell you where the Evil comes from."

"Where, Vegas?" Samuel laughed. It was such a cliché.

"I'm dead serious. McMannon interpreted the Indian name for Vegas as 'Sands of Fertility,' but it's a faulty trans-

lation. If he'd spent more time in the field he'd have realized that it's really 'Sands of Blood.' Hell, their oral tradition's full of warriors dragging enemies for miles just to kill
them on the Sands of Blood."

"Why?"

"To make sure that their bodies wouldn't contaminate
good land and, more importantly, to make sure their spirits
would know true pain."

When they reached Hoover Dam, Jerry parked on the
far side and together they walked back to the Nevada eleva-
tor tower. Jerry flashed a yellowed ID and the guard allowed
them to descend unescorted to the third and middle level,
one of several levels not included in the official tour.

Walking through musty access tunnels, the tons of
cement and water seemed to vibrate all around them, as if
the electricity came from the structure itself and not its gen-
erators. "I was here the whole time it was going up," said
Jerry, who was breathing harder for all the walking. "Pretty
amazing what us ants can do when we put our minds to it,
eh?" They had reached a sharp turn. Jerry pointed the flashlight around the corner and Samuel stopped dead.

A cast-iron staircase descended down into the rock as
far as the light's powerful beam could penetrate, stopped an
incredible distance down by a thick subterranean fog.
Samuel could hear a torrent of water falling even farther
below. Jerry turned the flashlight upward to show that the
staircase continued out of sight in that direction as well, in
a gentle curve that matched the contours of the dam's
Nevada slope.

Then the old man turned off the flashlight and the pair
were plunged into a kind of darkness known only to cave
explorers. The distant sound of the water mingled with the
old man's breathing like a thumb rubbing against a familiar
bruise. Jerry whispered. "Evil hates two things: Water and

Light. The dam uses one to make the other. A perfect match." Jerry switched the beam back on and aimed it right onto the seventh iron step leading down into the man-made abyss. "See that right down there? Look familiar?"

There, worked into the cold pattern of the metal, was the Sanskrit word for "soul." *Ka.* The prayer. Jerry's prayer, carved into the dam over fifty years ago. "Twelve words long. Repeats itself several hundred times. Arizona side, too, runnin' side by side. It'd be stronger if they crossed, but there was no place in the blueprint for that and I wasn't about to tell those engineer folks how to build their damn dam." Jerry laughed for the first time that evening.

"What's the prayer?" asked Samuel. Jerry just smiled, the echo of his laughter returning from the depths.

An hour later they were in Las Vegas, walking the Strip. Jerry pointed to samples of his work—at least one on each casino. Samuel was most impressed by the lollipop clutched in the hand of the eighty-foot Circus Circus clown. If he believed what the old man was telling him, it was more than neon. It was a mandala of spiritual power. Yin and Yang in neon and fluorescent.

"The lights. All the lights. They're just an extension of the dam, really. Look up and what do you see?" Samuel saw nothing. "The stars are still there. Just can't see 'em because it's between them and us." Samuel looked at Jerry. He was really serious. Evil—whatever the hell that meant— collecting in the sky above Las Vegas for decades, held in place by something as insubstantial as light? Pretty amazing concept.

What if it were true?

What would happen if it descended?

Inside the Sahara, they grabbed a beer at one of the bars. Samuel had avoided the casinos since he'd moved.

He'd been a sucker for the California Lotto enough times to know instinctively that he would get hooked if he wasn't careful, but it was different with Jerry around. It felt safe. The old man swept his hand to encompass the crowd.

"All this here's a side effect. It feeds off their greed and desire. That's okay, though. You think my puny efforts could keep it trapped up there if it were truly hungry? Even does some good. Most of these folks leave...empty. Heck, that's almost as good as cleansed!" he cackled.

On their way out, Jerry stopped at a dollar slot machine. "Let me show you something." He dropped in a dollar, pulled the handle and waited. The bells and the flow of coins seemed endless. When it finally stopped Jerry was two hundred dollars richer. Another dollar in another machine and the ritual repeated itself, this time with a three hundred dollar jackpot. Samuel was spooked.

Jerry smiled. "It's trying to bribe the warden."

Shortly before dawn, the two men climbed to the warehouse roof to finish off a six-pack. They'd done this often enough before, usually at the end of the week, but this time Jerry was far from relaxed. He sat motionless, staring at the distant city.

"I've been lucky," he sighed. "Sooner or later the lights're gonna go out. The prayer'll hold for a while but after that it'll all be lost. Everything. Can you even begin to comprehend that?"

Samuel could not answer him. He simply did not believe the old man, even though he sympathized. As a "sometime-Catholic" he rarely went to church. He didn't even pray much. By comparison, the years and effort Jerry had dedicated to his private faith were staggering. He had enclosed Las Vegas in a personal religion of light.

"Use the prayer. Make it stronger." Reluctantly, Samuel nodded. He could at least make Jerry happy by pretending to believe. The old man had tried to pass the flame on to his young apprentice and he had failed. Las Vegas was still just a city to Samuel. For Jerry, it was a holy fire.

The old man chanted his prayer out loud until dawn, at first in a language that Samuel could not recognize and then in English. Samuel listened, but he could not bring himself to join in.

That was eight years ago. Jerry had died three weeks later from a cancer he'd been nurturing quietly for over a decade. "If they cut you open it'll spread like gangbusters," he had wheezed to Samuel from beneath the oxygen mask, laboring with every breath. "Then you can't stop it." The funeral was small but dignified.

It was foolish for Samuel to have thought he could keep the old neon business going. Several clients used Jerry's death as an excuse to go with new and more modern companies. It was more than just a matter of his own inexperience. Something intangible had shifted with the old man's death. He felt…watched, scrutinized and studied by…it? No. He did not believe in Jerry's "prisoner." It was just his paranoia, he told himself—vibes picked up from clients sizing him up, trying to find out if he had picked up any of the old man's legendary talent with the glass. Even so, he found himself looking over his shoulder, completely on edge. Near the end he was breaking three tubes for every five he finished and of those five maybe three were good enough to send out. Then the banks took over the warehouse and the business was lost.

Only then did it reveal its presence fully to Samuel. He had been drinking most of the afternoon and on a fluke found himself walking the Strip, looking for samples of the old man's handiwork: a neon eye winking at him, dollar signs dancing above his head, the oscillating pink flowers of the Flamingo pulling his gaze upward into...the darkness. No matter how long he stared, the sky remained a fathomless black, as if stars had never been invented. A strong force was captive in Las Vegas. Whether it had been the old man's doing or not was totally irrelevant. The long rows of shining casinos seemed a poor defense against the tremendous weight of decades of nothingness.

Then he found himself standing in front of the Sahara, hypnotized by the bells and tones of the machines. On a whim he found the machines that had spit money for Jerry. *It's trying to bribe the warden.* He caressed the edges of the silver dollar before dropping it in and pulling the handle. While the wheels were still spinning Samuel had a sudden urge to leave, run from the casino as fast as he could, but he really needed the money now that his unemployment had run out. It was worth a try. Maybe he had inherited some of Jerry's power and the odds would tilt in his favor. Would Evil respect Samuel?

Several more times that night Samuel had put the question to Jerry's prisoner, first in the form of dollar slots and then on into the more expensive forms of blackjack and roulette. Evil knew Samuel was no warden and told him so with every losing bet. In less than two days it had swallowed his meager savings, leaving little more than a pittance with which to live off the fatty $2.99 buffets and the free well drinks that came when you sat at the gaming tables.

For six long years now it felt as if he'd been passing the same five-dollar chip back and forth endlessly between himself and the constantly changing dealer. In his mind he begged for the darkness to either finish him off or let him go and yet here he remained. Evil was not going to be that kind. And all the while Jerry's tubes were slowly disappearing from the casinos—victims of windstorms and fatigue, leaving the prayer to stutter its way around the city, incomplete.

As Samuel sipped his watered-down gin he contemplated the slot machines. Wasn't pulling the handle kind of like crossing oneself? Was there a difference between a roulette wheel and a Tibetan prayer wheel? Samuel imagined all the gamblers in Las Vegas as unwitting pilgrims, paying tribute to the imprisoned darkness, a tithe of greed pouring continuously into the sky...feeding it.

And then he heard about the problems at Lake Mead. The water level was dropping at an alarming rate, partly from drought and partly from an underground cavern that had opened up, channeling the water away from Hoover Dam. The engineers could not explain it.

It'll spread like gangbusters.

It would only take a minute—an unexpected break in the city mains, the neon pulling too much current on the back-up systems. Evil would carve a new branch into the Grand Canyon before picking up speed and covering the earth like a thick and deadly smog. Who could survive its fury? What mother wouldn't slit the throats of her children? What general wouldn't fire his missiles? Who would be saved?

Would Samuel?

He still had the prayer. He imagined himself floating in a little ball of serenity as the screams of the world tossed him and flowed past him, all the while muttering the old man's prayer to himself, hoarding it, saved and encased in its power.

May the fire of my soul be a shield against the darkness...
May the fire of my soul be a shield against the darkness...
May the fire of my soul be a shield against the darkness...

Joshua Mertz

Roadgod

from
1991

Joshua Mertz co-hosted all the parties from which this book is drawn. A natural storyteller, he is one of those people who puts an audience at ease with the sound of his voice (even at the same time that his story is unnerving them!)

The son of a rocket scientist and (in his words) "an extremely word-savvy mother," Joshua has worked as a printer, a TV switcher, a DJ, a screenwriter (for a cocaine smuggler!) and a teleprompter. His story "Cat Got Your Tongue" was published in Aboriginal Science Fiction, his poetry has been published in various magazines, including Harper's, and he recently completed his first novel, Machine Dreams.

I first heard about "Roadgod" when Joshua called me in early October of 1991 to tell me that he was going to write "a cyberpunk Halloween story" for the party. I was skeptical. It seemed to me that the genres were incompatible. Cyberpunk is all about technology and urban density. Halloween, no matter how you slice it, boils down to a celebration (or at least an acceptance) of Nature's cycle of life and death. I didn't think the styles would mesh.

You're about to see how wrong I was. "Roadgod" fuses genres by focusing on the religious nature of Halloween, and the universal desire to have a system of belief to explain the things, good and bad, that defy explanation.

A final caveat, though—this story is not for the squeamish. It will disturb you.

Roadgod

by Joshua Mertz

The accident happened literally before their eyes. The other men on the rugged hillside sat apart from Wexler. He was not yet part of the group. Before them the wall of the Eye-Ten Transportation Corridor stretched from one horizon to another painted with evening light; six levels high, twenty lanes wide, pulsating with the white noise of movement. The Shaman chanted along with the vibrating concrete, pulling a rhythm from the chaos, entreating the Roadgod. It gave Wexler the willies.

Then it happened. Before their eyes.

Fourth level, eastbound personal transport, fast lane: a sporty gadabout, trying to change lanes a bit too sportily at two hundred kilometers per hour, dodged in front of an accelerating family van and was broadsided by the larger vehicle. Other vehicles swerved expertly around them as the exchange of energy played its magic upon the situation.

The gadabout spun across the safety shoulder, smacked the outer railing at an oblique angle, and flipped end for end, flattening itself against a support pylon and bursting into flame. The van slewed drunkenly about in the fast lane before darting across the shoulder and bouncing off the railing. It rolled onto its roof, the windows shattering into clouds of scintillant white. Metal screamed on concrete as it ground to a stop.

Carrying rope and tools, the men ran toward the multi-tiered freeway. This was Wexler's first hunt, so he took up the rear where the Shaman had placed him. Fresh from the city and already out on a prowl. He was excited.

The enclosed lower deck of the Eye-Ten, the mass commercial level, thrummed with a percussive enormity that made conversation impossible. The catapult carriers assembled their devices. Grappling hooks and pulleys were tied to ropes. Wexler lifted and held things, feeling the Shaman's eyes on him.

The catapults were cocked, aimed, and fired, the grappling hooks caught the railing some thirty meters overhead, and the ropes were pulled tight. From the time the family van had impacted the gadabout, two minutes seventeen seconds had elapsed.

Men stepped into loops in the rope and others pulled them upward. Wexler was one of the pullers. Everything depended on time, they had said. The first five minutes were the most important; the accident victims' shock began to wear off after that. Wait ten minutes and the Highway Patrol copters would start arriving. The rope went light as the men at the top disembarked. The pullers let it fall to the ground.

To Wexler's amazement, the Shaman gestured him into one of the loops. Others got on the rope and they were jerked aloft.

The ground fell away and the rope twisted, swinging Wexler's gaze across the dark hills, campfires like glimmering stars, then a glimpse of the side of the Eye-Ten structure disappearing into the distance, then a bright vista of streaming vehicles under ghastly mercury vapor light, another glimpse of the flank of the freeway, then the dark hills again. He rose to the fourth level and rough hands pulled him into an unending explosion of noise and stench.

Wexler had expected loud and fast, but he had not imagined the enclosed pungent throbbing of level four. He ran to join the others busily dragging loot from the van.

He stooped to look into the inverted vehicle. Four passengers dangled in their safety harnesses, five if you counted the baby in its armored cocoon. The infant could be heard screaming through the plastic. The two adults in the front were unconscious or dead, their faces full of shattered glass. The woman in the passenger seat was pressed crazily against the crushed roof. Two children in the back seat. The little girl, her dress falling around her face, whimpered weakly, blood running down into her eyes. Her younger brother screamed and held his broken left arm, his eyes wide and unseeing. The scene did not shock Wexler. He had worked street accidents with a neighborhood gang back in San Frangeles. The baby stirred something in him, though. A feeling of loss that he automatically shunted aside.

Slinky Ted was inside the cramped quarters, extracting the dangling driver's wallet. The driver clawed at him and mouthed a sputtering plea for help into the overwhelming din. Slinky Ted slapped the driver to shut him up, then, for good measure, slapped the screaming boy. This only made the boy scream louder. Ted hit him again, harder, and the screams subsided to gurgling moans, lost in the traffic noise. Wexler accepted a booty bag and a small suitcase and ducked out of the stifling enclosure.

He ran to the edge of the roadway and cast his load into space. The Shaman was being helped over the rail, his eyes sparkling with excitement. Wexler trotted back to the van. Slinky Ted was rifling the glove compartment. The baby's protective bubble sat on the pavement among the detritus. Jeff and Rilke had the back door open and were passing luggage to carriers. They whooped with delight and pulled a medium sized dog from the wreck. It lay at their feet, dazed and frightened. Laughing, Rilke brought his boot down on the animal's neck and Wexler felt his heart leap.

Meat. He couldn't remember when he had last eaten meat. All eyes were on the kill.

Something at the corner of Wexler's vision caught his attention. The Shaman was gently lifting the baby from its protective bubble. The tiny face stared silently at the old grizzled one.

Jeff and Rilke ran with the twitching dog to the railing and threw it into the darkness. Packages were pressed into Wexler's arms and he, too, ran to the railing, freeing his load into space.

The others joined him at the edge, shinnying over the side and down the ropes. He swung over the rail as he had been taught, making sure he had a good grip. As the railing rose to block his view, he saw the Shaman holding the baby aloft, saw the man's lips forming solemn words. A pang of horror passed through Wexler as he saw the flash of the Shaman's arm and glimpsed the infant arcing out over the lanes of traffic. The railing rose and Wexler descended into the darkness.

Later that night, after a greasy meal of meat and rice, Wexler did not feel good. It was not the food. He sat away from the fire and nursed his sadness and pain.

The Shaman came and sat beside him. The Shaman had squinty eyes and affected a perpetual mock smile. "You did well," he said in a nasal voice. "The Roadgod is pleased."

Wexler snorted.

The Shaman squeezed Wexler's shoulder with two fingers.

"You saw my gift to the Roadgod. Every year at this time I keep my eyes open for morsels." He tapped the side of his nose. "I smell it in the wind."

Wexler turned angry eyes to the older man. "Don't smell shit, mon. Roadgod is stupid, hanker. Make it fo' a clam like you to try and be somethin' you ain't." The Shaman made no reply. "Stupid shit what you do witha baby," Wexler continued. He spat on the ground. "Malo."

The Shaman smiled. "We will talk later." He rose and ambled to the fire.

Wexler stared at the retreating figure, his heaviness unabated. Wexler was tough, wearing his indifference as a badge of manhood. He was, nonetheless, unwillingly visited by an image of the baby, a cry of glee or surprise on its tiny face, sailing toward its inertial transaction with the onrushing traffic. It bothered him, jarring loose another mental picture; not a baby, but a young boy. The boy was smiling at Wexler, trusting him.... He let the picture sink back into a sea of pain.

The others gathered around the Shaman as he produced a long pipe and several jars from his pack. Wexler wondered how these people had found one another. He himself was on the lam from the Hoover Bloods. Fallout of a deal gone bad. He had walked east out of San Frangeles for five days. No family to leave behind; no siblings that he could remember. Only a black door where brotherly love had been.

Then these guys, a hunting party from some tribe up in the hills, had taken him in and fed him. That was yesterday. Tonight there had been the hunt.

The Shaman lit the filled pipe with a stick from the fire and ceremoniously passed it to his right. It moved among the several men, each inhaling deeply and holding the smoke.

The pipe passed back to the Shaman, who refilled it with some leaf from one jar, some tar from another, a powder from a third. He rose and walked over to Wexler.

Wexler took the pipe and eagerly put it to his lips. The Shaman held the fire down and bade him inhale, looking into his eyes as the caustic smoke filled Wexler's lungs.

"The Roadgod is powerful," he intoned. "Without mercy. The source of life. Three is the number of its power. The Roadgod sings the song of songs forever." He stared thoughtfully for a few seconds as Wexler held his breath, then whispered, "We are all in the teeth of the Roadgod."

Wexler let the smoke out, coughing at its roughness, and the Shaman made him inhale more. The old man returned to the fire circle.

The acrid smoke burned as he exhaled through his nose. His focus went out, then back in, and his forehead tingled. Wexler put his arms around his knees and looked at the fire, waiting for a righteous buzz to come on.

It did not come.

He unwound his arms and looked up. The scene at the fire looked absolutely normal. The Shaman caught his eye, then looked away. Screw 'em, Wexler thought. Don't need nobody.

He got to his feet, walked into the darkness, and urinated into a bush. He continued uphill, over the shoulder of the wash.

Before him, over a kilometer away, lay the endless wall of the Eye-Ten, a horizon unto itself. To the right, San Frangeles hung in the haze of its own brilliance; to the left, the darkness of the desert. Across it all ran the jeweled serpent of the Roadgod. Its sides glimmered with moving headlights, its voice was a rumbling roar.

"You sho' big sumbitch," Wexler muttered to the distant wall of reinforced concrete.

The freeway rippled as if shaken by an enormous spasm.

A great hump ran down the transportation corridor, a wave from over the horizon. The earth shook with thunder, throwing Wexler off his feet. He looked up to see the freeway tremble again and pull itself loose from its moorings, leaving a track of broken pillars and posts. It lifted, snake-like, into the air, spewing speeding vehicles like flecks of rice. The great running structure rose higher and higher, falling back onto itself to crouch like a living thing. The torn concrete pinched and bulged and formed itself into a saurian face.

The face turned to look at Wexler. Wexler groveled and lost control of his bowels.

The huge serpentine form leaned closer, foul breath issuing from the twisted wreckage of its snout. "So," it rumbled, "you have come to me."

Wexler had no choice but to nod. He looked up into the looming visage. The Shaman had been right; very powerful, no mercy. The towering serpentine shape of concrete and metal, pulsing with bright life, studied him.

"Your brother wanted to die," it thundered. "He came to me willingly."

There exploded in Wexler's head a scene he had forced himself to forget. His younger brother, Benjamin—his best friend and confidante—running before the onrushing car of the dealers he had crossed. Watching past the gun in his face as his brother, legs broken, screaming for mercy, was thrown onto the freeway where he was crushed and battered into a red smear. Wexler's heart had shattered and he had felt as worthless as the drug dealers' sarcastic spittle soaking into the sidewalk. His brother. The person he had sworn to protect. Gone. The memory tore at him.

"He's all dead, mon." Raw-throated whisper in the night.

"Your brother gave his life to me of his own will," the saurian face boomed. "He served me well." It leaned closer, a crushed red automobile dribbling from its maw. "Now it is you who will serve me."

Wexler found his eyes brimming with tears. "Yes," he whispered. "Roadgod."

The next day, as dusk and the time for the hunt arrived, Wexler walked back over the shoulder of the wash and saw, exactly where the serpent visage had held its head, the crushed red carapace of a car. A thrill ran through his guts. It must have been real.

He took the Shaman aside and told him of his experience. The wizened man proclaimed the event prophetic.

He welcomed Wexler and said that he, Wexler, would bring luck to the day. The others also welcomed him and they sat in comfortable camaraderie on a hillside overlooking the Eye-Ten, awaiting the bounty of the Roadgod.

The Shaman sat beside Wexler, speaking of the history of the tribe, of the first three; the man who hunted, the woman who waited in the hills, and the living Roadgod. The Shaman spoke of the endless bounty of the Roadgod and the sacrifices that must be made to it.

Miraculously, it happened again in front of them. A van and a station wagon took their entanglement to the rail, rolling along the shoulder together like sparring animals. A cheer went up from the men as they ran downhill.

Wexler shouted the loudest and ran with the fastest, the wind warm in his hair, his legs tingling with excitement: he was honored to ride the rope up with the Shaman.

On the shore of the roofed river of speed it was a wonderment of chaos. The station wagon lay crushed up against the railing. One of his comrades had the back open already and was casting luggage onto the pavement. Two others ran to the railing with a struggling dog and launched it into the night. Another had the passenger door open and was searching the people inside.

The Shaman trotted to the van lying on its side and Wexler followed. The female driver had been dragged out and thrown to the tarmac. She screamed against the roar of the freeway and clutched at her chest. Someone was inside the van, throwing booty out the door. Wexler ran to help.

Over the top of the wreck he saw a small child dragging itself along the shoulder some twenty meters away, leaving a trail of blood. The child's torn clothing flapped in the wind from passing cars. Wexler sensed the Shaman beside him. The older man grinned broadly and gestured at the injured child.

In a flash, Wexler understood. Lost in vision, he felt his legs carry him toward the small form. He was the chosen of the Shaman, the blessed of the Roadgod, allowed to serve the living deity. He saw the life of the child before him, the life of the baby yesterday, the lives of all who consorted with the pulsating embodiment of transport, as mere drops of blood in the veins of a concrete universe.

He picked up the child and turned it around. It was a boy of five or six, his face scraped and raw. The front of his shirt had been torn open as if by great teeth and blood gushed onto Wexler's hands.

He ran with the screaming child back to the waiting Shaman. Wexler felt exalted. The shrieking child in his hands was his brother, everyone's brother, surrendered as the greatest gift to an overwhelming deity. He faced the cars flashing by and held the boy high.

The Shaman shouted solemn words, made the sign of three at Wexler's back, and shoved him into traffic.

Wexler's rapture crumbled with the realization of his betrayal. He was nothing more than a morsel to be thrown to their foolish deity. Stumbling into the fast lane, holding the writhing child with one hand, his body twisting sideways, Wexler tried to rise and run. He looked up to see the truck mere meters away and heard in the marrow of his bones the howling hunger of the Roadgod.

Christian Ulm

My Dinner
With Buck

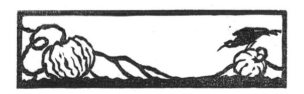

from
1989

For ten years Chris Ulm was editor-in-chief (and co-founder) of Malibu Graphics, the parent company of such familiar titles as Spawn and Men In Black. When Malibu was acquired by Marvel Comics, Chris left to co-found MainBrain Productions, an entertainment development studio with clients ranging from Klasky Csupo to Universal Cartoon Studios. Currently, Chris is writing and designing interactive entertainment for software developer Oddworld Inhabitants.

Chris's lifelong love of comic books comes through in his writing style, which reads like a hot mix of broad farce and old E.C. Comics gore. And, like Steve Taylor, he was someone you could count on to make you laugh. "My Dinner With Buck" was the first story Chris brought to one of our story parties and in many ways it's the funniest. In it, Chris gives a whole new meaning to the word "lovelorn."

My Dinner With Buck

by Christian Ulm

The saw bit into the corpse, then sputtered and died as the blade caught on the ribs and snapped off. "Dammit. Why does this always happen when I'm in a hurry?" I stared at the broken blade darkly. It was already six o' clock—an hour before I had to be at her house—and I wasn't even close to finished.

If I showed up late, I'd never hear the end of it. She didn't understand my creative drive. "You're always late," she'd say, stamping her foot daintily. "You never remember my birthday. All you seem to care about is your stupid hobbies. Well, I'm not like all those other girls always hanging on you! I'm not just some dumb nag you can *dissect* any old time you want to!"

Heather. I'll never understand her. Now she was noticeably cool to me. I even had to invite *myself* over for her family's annual Halloween dinner.

I sighed and concentrated on the matter at hand. Luckily, I had no more serious snags. I had the chest cavity exposed and the internal organs laid out in a jiffy, and within a few short minutes the heart was floating merrily in my own special "secret sauce" of formaldehyde and rubbing alcohol. Whistling cheerfully, I capped the jar and set it next to all the others on my "love shelf."

As I looked at its perfectly proportioned chambers and valves, I couldn't help thinking of her—the nights we had spent together, watching TV and holding hands, basking in the glow of our mutual love. Brushing away a tear, I placed the remainder of the body in four Hefty Bags—the ones with the neat plastic ties and reinforced seams. I'd mail them later.

A quick glance at the clock and I knew I was in trouble. Six-thirty…it was going to be close.

I snapped off the lights, threw my bloodstained smock into the Kenmore washer with the other whites, bolted the cellar door, and climbed up the rickety wooden stairs, flinging clothes every which-way. I showered quickly and pulled on my blue Bugle Boy trousers (with the really cool Velcro fly) and a white turtle-neck, leaped into my Reeboks and ran out the front door. The neatly clipped lawn looked lovely, although I nearly tripped over a headstone in my haste to reach the driveway.

I helped myself to a bouquet of white roses that were barely wilted at all (leaving the card behind, of course), climbed into the hearse, and smoothly pulled away from the old homestead after a quick personal hygiene check in the rear-view mirror, which loyally confirmed my irresistibility.

I should have realized something was wrong when I spotted the red Mazda Miata parked in Heather's driveway— right behind her father's blue Mercedes coupe. In *my* spot.

A jack-o'-lantern grinned smugly at me as I approached the thick oak door of their fashionable Spanish-style California home. The former pumpkin seemed to know something I didn't.

"Piss off, you stinking vegetable," I muttered under my breath, ringing the bell. When the door opened, I felt an explosion of excruciating pain as two-inch fangs sank into my leg.

"Reggie, you stop pestering," Heather's mother said, gently prying her son's head from side to side in an effort to remove his incisors from my leg. With a wet ripping sound Reggie came loose, a thick wedge of skin still between his teeth.

"Buck taught me that!" he said proudly, holding his trophy aloft. Reggie's face snarled into a smile and he wiped my precious bodily fluids from his mouth onto the undershell of his homemade Teenage Mutant Ninja Turtle costume. "Buck's a happenin' dude, man!"

"That's nice, Reggie. Run along now and put on the rest of your costume. It's tricks or treats after dinner." Mrs. Langdonsky, an attractive woman in her mid-fifties, regarded me quizzically. "What brings you here, Jack?"

"Who's Buck?" I demanded, trying to look over her shoulder and staunch the flow of blood from my leg in the same motion.

"Let me get Heather," she said, her face an unreadable mask.

I caught the delicate scent of broiled headcheese before the door shut with a final clunk. The smell brought back painful memories of better times, when this same woman was the mother I never had, making haggis and playing cribbage with Heather and me on rainy afternoons. Now she was a stranger—someone else was the object of her affections. I blinked back tears as the door reopened and a slightly disgruntled Heather appeared.

Large, doe-like green eyes and a slim but somehow voluptuous figure—my throat constricted in a paroxysm of agony. She wore a belted white dress which clung to her hips like Saran Wrap, revealing the barest hint of cleavage, a single rose in her shiny brown hair. The scent of lemon and honey assailed my nostrils. I was entranced.

"Are you listening to me, Jack McCann?"

"Hunh? Oh, sorry, Heather. What were you saying...?"

"That's one of your problems—you're always in your

own little world. I was *say*ing," she paused dramatically, "...that it's *over* for us. I just don't feel the same way about you anymore. You have to accept that."

"Who's Buck?" I charged belligerently.

"Nobody you know..." Reggie's delighted laughter emanated from somewhere inside.

"He seems to have made himself at home. Are you screwing him?"

She stiffened as if somebody had just connected a Diehard to her spine.

"Jack McCann! I hate you!" She tried to close the door, but I blocked it with my leg. The bad one. Black dots bobbed and weaved as a meat-cleaver of pain struck me between the eyes. Gasping, I fell over, the blood flowing again. I caught Heather's eye, silently pleading for her not to shut me out.

"Heather, I'm sorry—it's none of my business. Please forgive me. Can't we still be friends?"

She wavered, then smiled, opening the door a crack. "Okay, Jack. But that's *all* we are."

"Right. No problem. Now, how about dinner?"

"Oh, Jack, Daddy's not too pleased with you...and you and Buck may not get along."

"C'mon, this is the new Jack. I'll be a good boy— promise." I smiled endearingly.

She sighed. "Oh, all right. But remember, I warned you."

"What's *that* jerk doing here? He's a dork-face!" Reggie's nasal whine whipped through the suddenly silent room like a pistol shot.

The dining room looked just as I remembered it: ceramic dishes with the likenesses of all the Presidents in the china cabinet (except one—Reggie broke Eisenhower while chasing Seymour, his pet bat), wallpaper of multicolored ducks, Mr. Langdonsky's collection of semi-automatic weapons. Yes, the room was the same as always. Except for him.

Buck.

He sat to the right of Heather's dad (*my* old seat), a marked-up *Wall Street Journal* between them. He was dressed impeccably in the latest fashions from *GQ*—an understated, though elegant, wool sweater with creased trousers and shined Gucci shoes. The ensemble was capped by a thin aviator scarf, thrown around his neck in devil-may-care fashion.

He was also clearly dead—and had been that way for a long time.

"Jack is going to join us for dinner, everyone. Isn't that nice?"

Buck's watery eye sockets stared at me blankly, a piece of putrefied flesh creeping down his nose onto his plate. Without taking his good eye off me, he nonchalantly picked up the green matter and plopped it into his mouth.

"Well said, my boy!" Mr. Langdonsky chuckled, heartily clapping Buck on the back. "My sentiments exactly." He glared at me. "Can't you see where you're not wanted, McCann?"

Mrs. Langdonsky set a place for me at the table. "Now, now. None of that, dear. Jack is our guest. Let's remember our manners. And put away that newspaper. Honestly, your and Buck's financial talk will be the *end* of me."

"This boy's going places, I tell you," Mr. Langdonsky boomed, pointing to Buck as his wife cleaned up a stray bit of cartilage. "Why, if I'd had a *tenth* of this boy's drive when I was his age, I would be a millionaire today! Just as soon as these two kids tie the knot—"

"Daddeeee! Buck and I aren't even *engaged*..."

Buck took this moment to groan. A bubble of gas from his decomposing body sighed from his exposed trachea. Instantly, the room was filled with the stench of the dead.

"Aaaaaaaghhhhhhhhhheeeggggggg," Buck managed to say, bits of his fungus-encrusted lips forming a slow smile across his skeletal face.

"...*Yet*, anyway," Heather continued with an adoring giggle, her attention completely captured by this hulking corpse.

My heart sank. Clearly, she was in love. How could I compete with a man who wasn't even alive?

Mrs. Langdonsky set steaming bowls of headcheese for Mr. Langdonsky and myself, a hamburger patty for Reggie, a small vegetable salad for Heather and a live rat for Buck. Dinner was awkward, filled with pointed anecdotes about what a good fisherman Buck was, what a good dancer Buck was, how fast Buck's car went, how Buck saved the company thousands of dollars, how Buck showed the neighbors a thing or two about disciplining stray cats, how—well, you get the idea. It was over—I had lost everything.

I finished my dinner and excused myself. "I have to get up early and do some work. Thanks for a lovely evening. Don't eat anything you can't catch, Buck."

"Eeeeeaghhhhrrrrhhhhhahh."

Mr. Langdonsky lit two cigars and stuck one in Buck's mouth, popping out several teeth in the process. "Don't hurry back, McCann. My little girl has finally found happiness with this big lug here, and I don't want you to do anything to spoil it. Now go home to whatever it is you do, and leave her alone."

"Daddeee. I can take care of myself." Heather looked at me sheepishly. "I'll walk you to your car, Jack."

Reggie looked up, his cheeks full of barely cooked hamburger. "See ya later, Dickweed. C'mon, Buck. Let's play 'Buried Treasure.'"

The October air was laced with the smell of burning leaves and a full moon hung over Heather and me like a halo. "Sorry about Daddy," she said as we leaned against the hearse. "He's too protective."

"Don't worry about it." I looked into her guileless eyes. "Do you love Buck, Heather?"

"I'm pretty sure. He's passionate, kind, smart—".

"Dead," I interrupted.

"What's that got to do with anything? Can't two people with different backgrounds find love?"

"He consumes living flesh to survive!" I screamed, edging my hand closer to the open window of the hearse.

"I'm not saying there won't be problems. But I want to build a future with him, Jack. Besides," she said, her eyes twinkling, "being dead in bed *does* have its advantages…"

It was all too much. My hand grabbed the axe handle I always keep on the passenger seat and I dispatched her with one swift blow to the cranium. As I loaded Heather's crumpled form into the hearse, I felt a little sorry for her, but someone had to knock some sense into her. I hoped Buck wouldn't take it too hard, but, fearing the worst, I got out of there like a bat out of hell. Besides, they'd find her soon enough—I had the address memorized.

I cried with happiness all the way back to the lab. As I threw open the door to the basement, the jars on the shelves rattled and sloshed.

Boy, whoever said, "Home is where the heart is," sure said a mouthful.

Benjamin Gorman

Admonition

Admonition

by Benjamin Gorman

An orange sun descends like jaundiced eye
Into a tarry rheum of matted cloud;
A pale and sickly yellow smears the sky
And settles on the living like a shroud.

With eerie haste and silence of the tomb,
Black night descends—a brooding, noisome weight;
It spreads its petals like an acrid bloom
And pours like dark molasses, thick as hate.

Here, beneath this pall of ancient dark,
Foul denizens of nether worlds appear;
All manner, rank and feral, leave their mark
Upon the flesh of night, awash in fear.

This night is theirs to ravage and consume—
Great woe to souls caught helpless in its doom.

Now Darkness' minions hold their awful sway
And nameless creatures keep our world in thrall;
Now Light and Truth and Reason all give way
As Death's triumphant huntsmen sound their call.

Now on the march is Hecate's bloodless brood—
Her chaos-breeding army of the night—
Their captives, helpless, pitiful and nude:
The ghosts of soulless children, bound in fright.

Its demon's horns aglow in sulph'rous fire,
The sickle moon now plunges to the Earth;
Its fell intent, to spark a fun'ral pyre
Whose monstrous flames would wrap the planet's
girth.

So hearken, now, this warning that I give:
'Twere best all mortal souls should hide—and live!

Stuart Chapin

Bullfrog

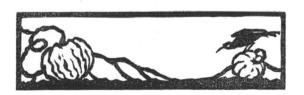

from 1992

My favorite story about a story is this: In the summer of 1992, Ben Gorman introduced me to his friend Stuart Chapin. Stuart was a fairly spectacular person to behold, standing about 6'5", with long flaming red-blond hair and high-intensity blue eyes.

Stuart is a screenwriter with an interest in horror, and so, sensing a kindred spirit and wanting some new blood, I invited him to write a story to read at our party.

The night of the party Stuart arrived late, snagged a glass of wine, and went back out to his car. His story wasn't done, and he had gone outside to finish it, tapping away furiously on a portable manual typewriter he had brought. At a certain point during the evening, I noticed Stuart come back inside with what I assumed was a finished story in his hands.

When it was his turn, Stuart launched into "Bullfrog." I remember that my reaction to the "new guy's" story was relief. It was very good—a creepy tale about a young boy and his twisted older brother playing a dangerous game on Halloween night.

What I didn't know was that at a certain point Stuart ran out of written material and improvised—making up the entire final third as he went along. No one knew—except one wide-eyed guest who was positioned in such a way that he could see Stuart run out of pages!

("Bullfrog" is also the most haggled-over story in the book. It had to be reconstructed from memory, you see, but that's another story.)

Bullfrog

by Stuart Chapin

The tunnel rolled onto Marv as Shell heaved up from his side and surged forward. The old nylon tunnel was not heavy except for the stench. But the wire that looped through it came down on Marv's arm like a rattrap sprung in slow motion. Marv lay pinned and gagging, face down on the dark drive. In about half a second Shell would swarm over and beat him so dead it wasn't funny.

Marv ooched back on palms and knees, leaving skin on the sharp gravel. He felt no pain, but the sour burn of fear was in his mouth. Fear has a tingling taste, like electrified copper pennies. Marv squirmed free and stood on tippy-toes. He still couldn't see over the tunnel. Shell was across it, flailing at it in his fury. On Marv's side, the enormous rancid hide pooched and rippled. Marv's heart hammered in his puny chest. Blood thudded in his ears. It was hard to hear exactly where Shell was at. The crumb-bum moved fast for a fat kid. Panic made the blood bang louder.

The tunnel was merely more Swap Meet trash was all— a long rotty tube of army surplus tenting. Its mouth yawned at the sidewalk and its tail went up the concrete slab porch to flop against the glass jalousies in the front door. Just a humongous old covered Slinky that smelled like mildewed socks and rotted birds. This year's haunted Halloween Tunnel of Doom.

One word croaked from the dark lawn. "Girly." Marv's legs and arms felt connected to him by broken rubber bands. He knew by heart all the words to the song Shell made up for beating on his face.

See the little girly,
Ball his girly fists,
Dudn't want no fightin',
Only wants a kiss!

For a long time Marv knew that Shell would kill him one day. The thing was bound to happen. One day Shell would sing and sing and just not stop. The only dull surprise was it happening tonight. Usually Shell was less antsy at night. But on Halloween, Marvy, all bets are off.

The plan had been to scare trick-or-treaters. The only way to the lit porch was through the Tunnel of Doom. But hidden by junk and darkness between the sidewalk and the house, Shell and Marv lay in wait outside the Tunnel. They were flat on their bellies opposite each other, Shell on the lawn and Marv on the driveway—their faces mashed blindly against the putrid nylon, their gloved hands thrust in through slits in the dank floor. So they waited, motionless as snakes. They waited for anyone to shuffle into the trap. Then they would grab them or trip them or spider-tickle fingers up a girl's bare leg. But no kids came.

"Shell?"

"*Tsst!* Shut up!"

"We got no treats."

"What?"

"At the house. No candy. Daddy kill somebody, knock at the door."

"Nobody gonna knock at no door, shut up."

"Well, it's the *idea*."

"I'll knock you. Knock your teeth down your throat."

"Shell?"

"WHAT?"

"Kids trick-or-treat and want *can*dy."

"Not if they never get that far. They get to us, wonder-brain. Use your head for more than a hat rack. They get to here in the Tunnel and we be on them like stink on shit. And you know what? It's *my* idea, so don't you tell me what's the idea. Now shut the F U dash dash up."

"I don't shut up I grow up and when I look at you I throw up."

"Yeah, you try it! I climb over this Tunnel here, Marv. I whup your ass for you two seconds and make you *eat* that puke you say one more word. And you know another thing? It ain't trick *and* treat is it? No. It's trick *or* treat. Fag moron."

"Shell?"

"Shut up fag moron."

"Am not a fag."

"Are too shut up."

They lay in wait forever and no kids came and no kids came. For a little while Marv put the gigglefits on Shell with a game of blind-man's slapjack. The unseen, workgloved fingertips brushed each other. But it didn't last. No trick-or-treaters came. Shell got bored out of his skull. No victims tried out his Tunnel of Doom. And things got awful antsy then.

Wade Nesfield, Sheldon and Marvin's daddy, considered his boys good enough boys so far as they went, like all other boys. They got whipped with a wide-buckle belt like all other boys when they went too far. Marv liked to be Mama's Precious Li'l Snotrag about lickings but Shell was getting so like a man it was scary. Wade did not care much to dwell on the niceties.

What Wade did care much for—and loved, if you wanted to use the word—were Swap Meets. His hunkajunk Pontiac was always first every blessed Saturday and Sunday morning to get into the Tropicaire Drive-In Swap Meet, just off the Palmetto Expressway at Bird Road. The funny part when you got down to it was that the Tropicaire quit showing movies about a decade ago. Speakerless speaker posts served as dealers' boundaries and tie downs for the tarpaulins that protected goods from sudden downpours. Most of all, the gelded speaker posts were linchpins between a Monday-to-Friday rutted parking lot's desolation and a weekend's bazaar of miracles and bargains.

Wade arrived first because pre-dawn hunts were the best. He would scuttle eagerly across the concrete knolls, sometimes in a loose pack of dealers, where each man would sweatily grip his niggerbag and swing the same powerful flashlight that had an underslung 12-vt. Delco battery. After checking out the U-Haul (nothing), the pack would have coffee and donuts in the concession stand. They would gather under the sign that for ten years said Next Week's Movie would be BLOOD BEACH and TOOTSIE and they would bicker and smoke and laugh raucously.

Some scrap—some *Sorry!* game taped shut or grocery bag of funnybooks—would always go home in the Pontiac. The rolling shitheap had needed a muffler about two Presidents ago so it was easy to hear coming. Its calamity of noise fixed Marv and Shell's weekend ritual into a lesser mirror of their father's. A ritual they menfolk thought of as fun and felt of as survival.

Shell raised holy hell on his side of the Tunnel—then abruptly he fell silent.

Marv had taken a single step to the house and now froze. Shell was listening for him. He was across the lawn and sneaking up the porch or down the sidewalk maybe to blindside him; Marv could not tell. Wind soughed through the Tunnel of Doom and flapped like a trapped bird in the sea grape tree. It was like a game of Psycho-rules *Battleship.* "Ain't funny, man!" Marv yelled, and sidestepped quickly. He scraped up gravel and lofted the pebbles over the tube. They fell without a sound and Shell never made a peep. At least *Battleship* gives out pegs to locate the enemy.

Marv stared at the long blind of tenting that stretched like the carcass of a monster worm. He was sorry daddy ever got this thing.

Every weekend morning the boys sat glued to cartoon shows and roughhoused and could not be budged from the teevee. Shell picked the shows and also the fights. After cartoons, there was *Tarzan Theater* on WCIX, Channel 6, and bloodshot eyes and complaints of headache. But like two puppets on one string, they would shake off (no ma'am) orders to scoot outside and play. They would sit and watch and wait.

At last, there would be a faint, angry rattle, like a yellowjacket in a mason jar. Then a six-cylinder fart would let go up the street and the boys would bang out of the house at a dead run race (whadjaget whadjaget?) because whoever got to daddy first got the choicest spoil of the hunt.

"Christ give me patience," said Darleen. "What did you drung home this time?" The Life's A Bitch And Then You Marry One woman in Wade's life said the same damn thing every weekend, and stood on the porch in housecoat and zoris with her arms folded the same damn way. And every weekend, Wade had to stand one foot out of the Pontiac and *explain* the bargain he lucked into. One fortunate Saturday in April, he had lives to explain, those lives the army didn't save when emergency tenting was left in their own lousy warehouse after a killer hurricane. Darleen swatted at a bootblack mosquito and refolded her arms. Wade explained about the 5½'-diameter tent's continuous single-coil ½" steel spring and its hide of practically not at all mildewed ripstop nylon. Then Darleen said the other same damn thing she always said: "Not in my house."

"I was only hoping to save our lives, like it matters," said Wade. "I am sorry. I apologize for loving my family. But if that's wrong, I'll try and do things more your way from now on."

"No daddy," pleaded Marv, tugging on Wade's WILL WORK FOR SEX tee-shirt.

"Here's what, Dar." Wade snapped his fingers even though they were too oily to make a sound. "Got this sunnabitch on top the car, I'll go to the dump now and pitch it. That make you happy? Speaking of dump, why not I take a crap in my wallet while I'm at it? Hunh? Or let me in the house a second and see what else we got from the no-good swappy meet. Like the teevee and them teevee tables and about the whole fucking place!"

Darleen went in and slammed the door and the glass slats rattled. His mood shot to hell, Wade rolled their salvation in the wake of a killer hurricane against the house and forgot about it.

Shell was on the move. Marv couldn't think how long it had been since he heard Shell make any sound at all. But now he was going to and fro on the lawn and walking up and down on it. The longer Shell stayed quiet, the worse got the beating after. Shell calling him swear words would be safer than this. Marv shot a glance at the porch. He could make a run for it and push aside the Tunnel and get in but if the door slammed shut, he'd catch hell. Daddy had a thing about that, but escape from Shell was worth the risk. If he knew what kind of a head start he had. If he had any at all.

"This was your idea, Sheldon, I hope you know," he called. "You better quit it. Warnin' you. You want to do this, then you want to lie on the ground then, I'm serious. Shell? Okay, just for that, I'm goin' in!"

The quiet crunch of footsteps. Where?

"I'm tellin' dad!"

Steps. Silence. Then again.

"Swear to God, I'm headin' in the house!"

He dared not move.

The Nesfield residence looked like a dog on a freeway shoulder—likely to die and like most of it was already dead. Essential difference between it and roadkill was that the house had years and years to suffer.

A wrought iron fence with a gate off its track fronted the property. Fleur-de-lis spikes topped the fence and rust made them blossom into delicately flaked orange flowers. Nothing else grew the same size. The lawn would be bare in one patch and knee-high sawgrass in another. Plants that survive on coral rock betray a tottery, urgent excess of life despite mortal disease. The lot was littered besides with half-begun projects, disused tools, broken BB rifles and worthless crapola. Whole armies of toy soldiers were lost on this battlefield, their graves unmarked. A weed-choked cairn of building bricks wore a yellow hood that was once a Slip 'n' Slide.

On hot days, which were most days, all the windows were cracked open. The baggy screens had never been replaced, let alone cleaned, and had so much give and grit in them that cross-drafts caused them to slap against the jalousies' edges with the jarring *ting* of wire on glass and then fill lazily outward with breeze. Marv imagined the belling screens were black sails unfurling that might some-

how unmoor the house and sail it to a place where everybody would be okay and not holler no more.

To Shell, the screens had nothing more in them than
palmetto bug poop. Shell was fourteen and his gutwad was
as hard as an egg of Silly Putty. He could get stinky finger
off of Maria Alvarez anytime and soon he bet she'd go okay
when he went could they ball and then there would be
nothing more to being a man. For Christmas he wanted his
own Mossberg shotgun and Wade had gone we'll see.

But Shell felt keenly the pull of magic. He rescued the
sack of tenting that leaned upside the house. It put him in
mind of the movie where the men wore spacesuits and E.T.
was dying in the house and nothing could be done. Shell
felt so awful at that part he wanted to die himself. He cried
as bad as all get out. Darleen let him a taste of the back of
her hand and Wade hissed was he a turd burglar sissy, but
Shell went on bawling and couldn't help it. Afterwards,
Wade showed a sense of humor off the issue. He brought
home swap meet dresses awhile and standing in movie lines
asked real loud did his oldest son need a kleenex or a tam-
pon? That Shell loved *E.T.* in spite of all was his worstest
shame and his bestest pride.

E.T.'s tunnel was clear and full of light, while theirs was
less see-through than dogshit and stunk like birds flew in it
to go home to Jesus, but that was no matter. Shell got to
use the tenting for Halloween, and never had to tell nobody
what it meant to him.

Marv had been to church twice in his life, on back-to-
back Sundays when Aunt Betsy from out by Pensacola
stayed with them. Marv fidgeted through the sermon and
didn't know the songs any. But he recognized prayer. He
saw women around him with their eyes closed, their dou-
ble-chins tucked on their bosoms and their hands clasped so
tightly that the charm bracelets could not jingle. He beheld

their faces and understood what Shell used to do after school in the tenting that leaned against the house. Shell didn't go to sneak mom's Kools or choke the chicken or catch Marv spying on him. He only sat and looked sad.

On these afternoons, sunshine pushing through the nylon bled green light on Shell's shaded face. He was the same color as the tenting, almost a living part of it. When he would rise up, he would walk stiffly to and fro and have the look on him that scared Marv half to death.

Wind rustled the sea grape tree. Traffic swooshed along distant 147th Avenue. There was no other sound. Maybe Shell had snuck inside the Tunnel of Doom. Maybe he was in there now, just sitting. He could be watching Marv's every move through some hole. Hoping for Marv to poke his arms inside, like before. Maybe even in the darkness green light was bleeding all over Shell's face.

Icy ridges of gooseflesh speckled Marv's skinny arms. "Hear me, now? I'm headin' in the house now, okay," Marv shrilly threatened the wind. "You A-hole!" He shut his mouth with a click and strained to listen. *I won't cry*, Marv instructed himself. *But scared Jesus I'm scared almost to pee my pants.* "Hey, booger-head, deaf or stupid?" he shouted aloud. "You rotten shit for brains! Lardass! Fag!" he sang with defiance and broke into giggles. Dad called Shell this stuff all the time and dad always laughed, but not like this. Never like this. Marv's laughter was wound up loopy. He wondered if Shell would think to clamber over the tube itself, squashing it flat and coming within a scarce lunge of—

"Double A-hole, fat, *pizzaface fuck!*" Marv was shocked twice, first to hear the words and then to realize that he had said them. Calling Shell fat was kind of asking for it, but to rank on his zits meant practical suicide.

One time Shell found a big as all bullfrog back in with the family lawnmowers and hedge clippers. After the both of them threw enough pebbles to see was it alive, Shell fetched a half gallon tin of Reddi-Lite kerosene from a shed. The tin sloshed heavily and Shell carried it with both hands. He walked stiffly and had the look on him. A watchful look that never cares one way or another about what it sees. Shell dirtied his shirt untwisting the rusted tin cap. "Just for that, sucker," he told the bullfrog, and he poured out all there was. As the kerosene *plooshed* and threw up fumes, the sides of the tin went in and out like the can was breathing.

Shell went into the house to boost some matches and Marv stayed with the glistening bullfrog and begged it to cross to the Torres's property. The bullfrog shifted its weight and Marv never knew such wild hope and happiness. Then Shell came back and lit a match and dropped it. The bullfrog found itself in a sudden pond three feet around and five feet up of all fire. Shell kicked its butt to make it hop while it roasted to death. But the bullfrog wouldn't move for nothing. It just squatted down and died.

A tear plodded down Marv's cheek and dislodged a speck of gravel. The boy shivered in the sharp October night. "Shell? Here's a last chance, 'kay? You go on your side and I go on mine and we start all o—" *Slap!* The tenting jumped and jiggles seesawed through it. *This is it oh God here he comes!*

But the Tunnel of Doom settled and Marv found that he had peed himself just a little. He could not stop the shivers. His legs went like a sewing machine and one was hot down to the knee. The truth merely was that Shell had hit the ground on his side and hit the tube getting there. Marv prayed *hail-Mary-in-first-place-blessed-are-thou-and-them-*

other-women like a shot. He heard dirt scrunch in the
unseen lawn. That would be Shell clumsily fitting his big
arms through the holes they cut. Marv dropped to his
knees. Hot, fresh tears squirted out shamelessly. He eeled
belly first opposite Shell and put his arms through the holes
on his side. Shell was back on his side; they were back where
they started. A thought tickled unpleasantly. *Did Shell
remember to give the knife back to mom?*

"Dumb A-hole," Marv whispered, and reached for his
brother...

Then Shell's gloved fingertips skimmed the back of his
hand and Marv felt a goose walk over his grave. *In Psycho-
rules Battleship the pegs you use come from mom's kitchen.* The
same, slow touch found Marv's other hand and Marv struck
back quick as a coral snake. The slapjack war was on. There
were no gigglefits about it this time. Gloved hands on the
tunnel floor twisted blindly and pinched and fought. Above
them, the nylon hide shook. Grunts and swishes echoed
through the tube's innards and made the monster come to
life and hungry. Shell was in the Tunnel, Marv realized; it
ate him already and wanted more. Marv's nose pressed into
the rotty old belly of the living worm. Any second it would
sense him. Its saggy mouth would recoil from the sidewalk
and swallow him whole. Blind, green graspers thrashed
inside the worm, knowing that part of Marv was in there
somewhere.

Shell reached more than ever, with arms that seemed
twice as long. The heebie-jeebies seized Marv first. His
arms spazzed on him, laying like dumb sticks that grew
from his shoulders. Shell could catch on them easy and haul
Marv face down and face first over the rough drive into the
sharp and corroded curl of wire, into the eaten away ripstop
nylon. Into the beast that would chew him to bits.

"No, I don't wanna!" a voice squealed.

A girl's voice.

Marv flinched and his fist coming back smacked his own face through the nylon. He was too startled to cry. Actual, honest to God trick-or-treaters were in the Tunnel of Doom.

"Lori, wait up. Wait up! I hate this place." The one in front, Lori, she whirled and went "boo!" and her friends screamed happily.

Marv held his breath, his arms dark and flat as mud on the floor. He caught back a moan as the Tunnel of Doom began to glow from within. A dim, orange moon bobbed through a storm of slashed green clouds. Someone inside had a light.

"P-U," said a girl and "Shh!" said another. The kids shuffled bumpingly toward the porch-lit door

(*"Trick-or-treat trick-or-treat"*)

and Marv watched their hunched-over silhouettes

(*"give me something good to eat"*)

swell crazily in the worm. Then the shadow behind their shadows rose up from the lawn. The shadow of his brother roused itself impossibly huge as the victims stepped within reach.

It's not him! Marv thought in crazy, sudden terror. *The monster's alive!* The girls went "What's that?" and "Who's there?" and the thrasher struck them. Bodies in the tunnel flew into each other and all the collision landed on Marv's head. There was no light, no air. The worm shifted and chewed. Noises fell like the spatter of rain on plastic. Everybody's screams were on top of each other, and were on top of him.

"Stop, stop!" Marv yelled. He drew up his knees reflexively. Girls kicked like maniacs, but if Shell had got hold of one, no way would he let go. Marv pistoned his legs with all his strength. The world above him tilted and split.

Ripping thunderclapped in his ears. He burst through and saw kids spill from the Tunnel to the street wailing like banshees. They ran scared as hell but Marv didn't laugh one little bit.

He sat up feeling sick, like after playing in rough waves at the beach. It took a second to work out that he was completely inside the Tunnel of Doom for the first and only time of his life. Shell's holy place was as weirdly hushed as he imagined it to be. Screaming kids and cars and wind were only muffly sounds, far away. Broken beside him lay a blue flashlight with an orange plastic jack-o'-lantern hood. Marv looked at it and was suddenly sick of Halloween. He got up to go to the house without even saying he quit. Shell was a fag moron and his Tunnel of Doom was lousy tenting was all, that even the Army was to throw out. Shell could come in when he pleased or lay out all night by himself.

Marv heard the echoey crunches of Shell walking again on the lawn and he knew what that walk looked like. But Marv had enough head start. He went blindly, his own footsteps crackling, until he kicked the porch and stepped up. Most Florida glass doors open outwards, but the Nesfields's was a Yankee door and opened into the house, so the tenting was flat against it. Marv was home free, his hand on the knob. He turned back for one last look.

And saw that he had tread through a goldmine of treasure. Light from the house shone and glittered on strewn candy. Clawed open loot-bags lay abandoned halfway down the Tunnel. Cellophone rolls of SweetTarts sparkled in the murk.

Marv waited, listened again for Shell but heard only the tenting's muffly echo. He hunkered down. After ten seconds, he crept to a packet of Whoppers. Nobody jumped him. He inched off the porch, still safe and sound. The place they set the trap was ankle deep in candy. Marv reached and took Baby Ruths, Milk Duds and Hershey's Kisses. Even with his hands full, Marv went just a little further to get more. He wasn't scared.

Or alone.

The man entered the Tunnel of Doom from the sidewalk. He blocked its mouth so fast and completely that street light only scraped around him. It glinted off the aglet in his bootlace. And another glint off something in the man's fist.

Marv turned and bolted. He forgot there was a door to his house, banged into the slat jalousies and bounced off. No glass broke by sheer miracle. Marv rushed the door again and burst inside. If the thing slammed he never heard it.

Wade and Darleen were finishing supper. Wade sopped meat juice with a cathead biscuit and washed it down with Pepsi. Marv stammered come quick there was a man out front and Shell went crazy. He grabbed some girls.

"Who grabbed some girls?" said Wade.

"Shell."

"God damn."

Wade went to the door and shoved away the tenting. "Shell! Get here now!" Shell didn't come, but that was no surprise. Marv was the baby and fussing the baby was cause for a whipping. "God *damn*," said Wade again, and flicked open his buckle with a practiced hand. The metal made a thrilling musical sound. "Stay here," Wade ordered. But Marv hung at his side by hooking a finger through a belt loop. So together they found Shell, or mostly found him, in the crook of the sea grape tree.

Marv's throat was raw. No one had listened to him talk this much his whole life, especially no grownups. The blankets on him were hot, but Marv was afraid the police would be mad if he took them off, so he just sweated. He told about the leaky Winn Dixie bag by the fence. It had Shell's head in it crookedly and there were Goobers and Kandy Korn in Shell's mouth.

"The tunnel rolled onto me one time. Think that was it, sir. That must be when he took him. I only heard…no, I didn't even hear a voice, correctly. But Shell's always playin' kinda crazy tricks. This was just like, here goes again. So I went, 'Y'all quit it, boy, or I beat you good.' And maybe it scared him. He couldn't see me, neither. We both got down and, alls was, we touched hands. I never saw his face. Sir, I can't tell you nothing about who he is or why he done it except…"

"Except?"

"Maybe Shell just looked like something he didn't like."

John Taylor and Jodi Taylor

Love is Where You Find it

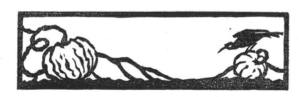

from **1993** Sometimes the way a story is read is as important as the story itself. Obviously, we couldn't let our memory of a great reading be too strong an influence when we chose stories to put into this book. We had to assume that a lot of people would read this silently. Still, sometimes you can't resist.

John and Jodi Taylor had just started dating when we threw the first of these story parties. By the tenth one, they were married and expecting their first child. John, along with his brother Steve, is a full time musician, and Jodi got her degree in drama at USC. Both of them are natural entertainers.

"Love Is Where You Find It," like all their stories, was a team effort both in the writing and the reading. The two would arrive at the party with their story marked up with several colors of highlighter pen, and proceed to play all of the various parts (invariably a man, a woman, a narrator, and some background personalities) with all the appropriate accents, sound effects and primal bellows.

"Love Is Where You Find It" is good, tacky fun no matter what, but if you really want to enjoy it, find a partner and read it aloud to some friends on Halloween night.

Some dishes are best served hot.

Love is Where You Find it

by John Taylor and Jodi Taylor

Everyone called Wendel Jeffries 'Rod'. Wendel knew well and good that 'Rod' was short for Nimrod but he liked the masculine sound of it nonetheless so he never protested. Not that he ever protested anything. In fact, Wendel often said, "My friends call me Rod." Not that he had any friends.

It was 11:45PM on Halloween night and all was quiet at the Brotman Medical Center morgue. Not that it ever got too noisy there. And that was the way that Rod preferred it. Working the graveyard shift gave Rod ample opportunity to read *PC World* and create Dungeons & Dragons characters with only the occasional clerical responsibilities to disturb his pursuits.

Tonight was such a night. Only two bodies had been brought down. One beating victim and one which the orderly only described as "a tragic trash compactor accident." Rod wasn't looking forward to the usual tag and bag duties for that one so he postponed them both knowing that the coroner wouldn't arrive for another eight hours.

The irony of working the graveyard shift in a morgue on Halloween night did not escape Rod, but he also knew that he didn't have any other real offers on a night when everyone else was at parties.

Rod could be best described as misshapen, which may account for the fact that he was assigned to the morgue when he first approached Human Resources. They didn't exactly want him having a lot of contact with the living.

His head was disproportionately larger than his body and was most unfortunately covered in a mass of strange, neither straight nor curly brown hair. But perhaps the biggest tragedy was that he didn't appear to have a real neck to support such a large head. He liked to think that his head was large because his brain was large and not because his mother had worked with caustic home improvement chemicals during her pregnancy.

The worst problem with Rod was that he'd had growing spurts which had started at the age of nine and had continued on until last year when he turned thirty-five. The victims of that final spurt were his feet, which, next to his head, were the largest part of his anatomy.

It was nights like these when Rod would become lost in thought about himself, his situation and the unfairness of it all. He was so deep in thought that he didn't hear the voice at first.

"Is anyone there?"

"Hello?"

Rod glanced over towards the entrance. Probably some grieving relative trying to give another last goodbye to their dearly departed.

"You can't be down here now. Come back at nine A.M."

"Where is here?" The voice was not coming from the door after all. It was coming from somewhere inside the room.

Rod looked around. "Who is that? Who's there!" He couldn't help it; his heart began to pound anxiously.

"Elizabeth," the voice said. "Elizabeth Myers."

Rod could feel the muscles in his back begin to stiffen as the reality of the situation hit him: the voice was coming from one of the two bodies laid out on the table across the room. Nervously, Rod pushed aside his Dungeons & Dragons Monster Manual and accidentally spilled his 7-Eleven Big Gulp as he scrambled for the paperwork on the two corpses. There, at the top of the second page, it read:

Name:	Myers, Elizabeth
Ethnicity/Gender:	Caucasian Female
Age:	29
Probable Cause of Death:	Complications due to severe head trauma

Slowly, the blood began to return to Rod's face. It was the assholes from upstairs, trying to pull another trick on him.

"Fuck you, Larry!" he shouted into the air.

"Excuse me?" the voice responded.

"Ha, ha, very funny," said Rod as he got off his chair. "Now I'm going to walk over to the sheet, pull it back, and hardy-har-har won't you get a big laugh." Rod stomped over to the Myers corpse and pulled back the sheet. But instead of finding Larry or Hector, the dickhead orderlies, there lay a female corpse. Rod looked away.

"Okay, guys, where are you?"

"Where am I?" said the body. Rod screamed and fell back, slipping in the already-spilled Big Gulp, and crashed to the floor. Elizabeth slowly propped herself up on one elbow and looked down at the terrified man.

"I'm, uh, you, uh, where, uh, what, uh…" Rod stammered. He was having a hard time getting it together. Elizabeth looked away, studying her surroundings.

"Am I in the emergency room?" she asked.

"No…" Rod managed.

"Is this the hospital?"

"Yes."

"Are you my doctor?"

"Not really."

"Am I okay? I mean, my head hurts. What's wrong with me?"

Rod got back on his feet and grabbed the paperwork on Elizabeth Myers. "Well," he said slowly, "it says here that you're dead."

"Dead? Am I really...dead?"

"Well, I guess not," said Rod.

"Well then, where am I? What's going on?" Elizabeth began to cry. Rod took a few cautious steps toward her, and awkwardly put his hand on her shoulder. It was warm. And it was soft. In fact, now that Rod wasn't so freaked out, he could see that she was strikingly beautiful, perhaps the most lovely woman he'd ever seen. He could tell she had gorgeous red hair, though most of it was sticky with blood, and big, soft green eyes.

"Hey, don't cry. You're not dead, really. I'm alive and so I would know. I mean, they thought you were dead. You were brought into this hospital with a head wound and I guess they thought you were dead, so they took you down here to the morgue. But obviously you're not dead anymore, or you never were or something. What happened to you?"

Elizabeth hesitated. "I don't even know how I got here. The last thing I remember, I was on the floor, trying to get away from him. He must have hit me with something from behind, I don't know. Next thing I know, I'm here."

"Who?" asked Rod. "Who was hitting you?"

"I'm cold."

"Here," said Rod, taking off his white work coat, "you can have my jacket." He put the coat over her bare shoulders, noticing for the first time that she was naked. Actually, all bodies down here were naked, but this one was alive, and that made quite a difference.

"Thank you," she said. "What's your name?"

"My name is...Wendel. My friends call me...Wendel."

"Thank you, Wendel."

"You're welcome…Elizabeth." The two sat there awkwardly for a moment. Rod was not used to being alone with pretty women, let alone one that would talk to him. Finally, he looked at her and said, "Maybe we should call someone and let them know you're alright."

"No…I mean, can't I just stay down here with you a while, Wendel?" She looked at him, her eyes brimming with tears.

"Sure, I guess." Slowly, Elizabeth leaned the uninjured side of her head on Wendel's shoulder and quietly wept. Wendel felt his hands begin to shake, but somehow managed to reach around Elizabeth's shoulders and hold her gently. They sat that way for several moments. Wendel liked it. Glancing down, Wendel noticed the ring on Elizabeth's left hand.

"It was your husband," he said. "Your husband tried to kill you."

"He's not my husband…yet."

Wendel felt angry.

"Does he do this a lot?" But Elizabeth said nothing. Wendel held her closer. "Well, if I were your boyfriend I would never in a million years hit you. I would treat you like a queen. How could anyone beat a beautiful woman like you? Some people just don't know how lucky they are."

Elizabeth stared deeply into Wendel's eyes.

"When I was a little girl, I used to dress up like a bride and I would wrap a towel around my head and pretend that it was a veil. I would usually marry one of my stuffed animals or I would picture in my mind a kind and gentle man all dressed in white who would take me somewhere very beautiful…I guess that was pretty dumb, huh?"

Wendel at that very moment felt like kissing Elizabeth's

round lips. The feeling was overwhelming and he could feel his face blush with heat.

"I don't think that's dumb at all. I think that it is beautiful. Just like you."

"Wendel, I know this is going to sound very strange but I feel as though I could tell you anything. I feel as though we are very old friends and that I could trust you. Thank you for listening to me. You are very kind."

Elizabeth leaned into Wendel and kissed him softly on the cheek. Drawing back, she locked eyes with him. Wendel was beginning to have feelings that he had never felt before. His body was warm and strangely tingling. He cupped Elizabeth's face in his large hands, awkwardly brushing some sticky strands of hair from her face. At that exact moment in time, Wendel felt love. He pulled her face to his, kissing her fully and passionately on the mouth. Elizabeth responded with equal passion.

Wendel had heard that people who had suffered traumas were emotionally susceptible but his body was not listening to what his mind was telling him, and he pulled her slowly down onto the table, pushing aside the white overcoat. Although he did not have any experience with touching a woman, his fingers and hands seemed to know what to do and Elizabeth's body responded. She fumbled with the buttons on his work shirt and their passion became more frenetic.

They soon became a stew of arms and legs and Wendel's clothes were thrown about the room. She guided him inside of her. Wendel moaned with the anticipation that can only be felt from thirty-five years of involuntary celibacy. He felt powerful and strong. His senses were alive and he could feel the heat of Elizabeth's skin. He could smell the sweet aroma of their sweating bodies. He could hear the pounding of their hearts. The pounding had a rhythm all its own. The pounding became louder, it filled the room with noise.

"YOU...SICK...FUCK!!!!"
"JESUS CHRIST! HECTOR, GET HIM OFFA THAT BODY!"

Wendel felt the hands of the orderly around his chest, pulling him from Elizabeth.

"No! What are you doing? I love her!"

"You are one sick fucking bastard. I always knew that you were a sick little fuck. I should just fucking kill you right now. What the fuck do you think you are doing fucking a dead chick?"

Rod squirmed to get out of Hector's grasp. "Elizabeth, tell him you love me. Tell him how much you care about me. Tell him how you said that I was your old friend."

The three of them stared at the lifeless blue cold corpse lying on the table.

Larry leaned in close to its face. "Yeah, Elizabeth, tell us all about it.... Hey, Rod, you stupid fuck, she ain't saying much. Maybe it's because she is dead and you are a psycho motherfucker. Hector, get him the fuck out of here before I fucking puke."

Hector dragged Rod's screaming body from the room. "Elizabeth! *Elizabeth!!!*"

Larry picked the sheet up from the floor and began to cover the corpse. Its legs were broken at the pelvic bone and dangled off the side of the gurney. With a little effort, he was able to put the body back in position and cover it up.

But as he left the morgue, Larry couldn't erase from his mind the image of what appeared to be a trace of a satisfied smile on the face of the dead woman.

Edith Weil

A Cross at the
End of a Circle

from 1993

What is Halloween? How did it start?

I have a friend who collects antique Halloween decorations, and it is fascinating to look at his collection and see the styles and perceptions of the holiday change over time. In the early part of this century, there was a strong emphasis on witches and cats, and they were drawn with sharp jagged lines and a real intent to scare—all hooked noses and slitted green eyes. Fifty years later those same icons were drawn as cute and cuddly. Times change. Perceptions change.

In this next story, Edith Weil took a departure from the modern, urban world to look back to a Halloween long ago and a witch who is swimming against history's tide, a woman who insists on remaining rooted to the Earth when everyone around her has begun to look up to the heavens. It is from this story that we plucked our catchphrase, 'Now is the time when the veil between worlds is thinnest.'

Times change. Perceptions change. "A Cross at the End of a Circle" is a beautiful and wistful glimpse of a time when traditions faltered, and wondrous things were lost.

A Cross at the
End of a Circle

by Edith Weil

In a hidden clearing they hoisted the likeness up on a sturdy
pole, ready to be carried. The torso's straw stuffing poked
through a skin of raggedy discards. His face peeked out
from behind a mask of oak leaves, and from his open mouth
shot a tangle of leafy branches laden with acorns. Wildly
magnificent he appeared, the effect heightened by the
horns protruding from his mangy head. His eyes were fits
of black sewing—angry, sad, or laughing, however it was
you looked at him. Around his neck hung strands of dried
flower necklaces made by the marriageable girls as parting
gifts. Encircling his head, a leafy wooden crown of oak.
From his waist protruded a large stiff phallus stuffed with
dried mint and seed and from there hung two sacks stuffed
with small onion bulbs. Sweet sage, lavender and rosemary
filled his head. He was, for the moment, a glorious king, a
fearsome warrior, ardent lover, and a passionate, tragic
hero. He was the Færie King, ruler of the natural kingdom.

Agrippina Serafina Thumbelina Greenapple—Aggie—
watched her creation hoisted into the air, legs dangling,
thinking she should have taken more care with his eyes, for
something about them wasn't quite right. They seemed
fixed on her whenever she glanced toward the looming
beast-man. Were they more familiar than usual, or perhaps
too distant? No matter. After sundown, he would be
gone—driven down for the winter, as it must be and always
was.

115

Heaps of wood were piled onto a cart for the evening's bonfire, along with a sack of apples to bury under the earth, later to feed the departed souls. The adults numbered six and one more was arriving. As night fell they would march to the old Stone Field; now in secret, though not always so—for who had put those stones there so perfectly for just this night?

Dark cloaks would cover their bodies as night's dark cloak wound round their secret meeting place. One had to be careful. As it was, several had opted not to join them this year, and several sent relatives in their place to keep the tradition but would not come themselves for they now held places in government or in the church and would not bear risking their futures to favor the past. This night, no longer free to them, had fallen to those who toiled long in the field, for what had they to gain from the God of the Jews and His Son?

Still, they took measures. Any brave soul venturing out this night would behold a march of Goblins and Pixies, the frightful carved faces of gourds and turnips: the souls of the dead, risen to walk the earth.

Three little children, siblings, if she could remember correctly, played dare amongst each other, each taking turns standing before The Green Man's frightening visage until his gaze became too much and they would run laughing and screaming, then push another one toward Him.

"Hello! Greetings. May I approach?" A figure stood halfway down the slope waving an arm at them.

"Who might you be?" shouted one of the men.

"Weylin, son of Aldo, the spice seller," he answered.

Two men went down and talked to the stranger, and soon returned with him, indicating assent with furtive nods of their heads to the group. He was a young man with a handsome face, neatly built, whose fine clothes bore hardly a wrinkle from his journey. Aggie saw the father in the son, but this one was not as the old merchant had been. This one had the manner of the new ones: friendly enough in face, heavy in kind words, practiced at manners (the things they learn in cities), lean in heartspace, ignorant of honest action. She was surprised to see him here.

"For two nights and three days I've traveled," he began, to nobody in particular, eyes searching the group for a likely authority. Finding none, he spoke to them all. "My father has passed away. At his behest, I've come in his place. It was his final wish." Weylin withdrew a cloth-wrapped bundle from his sack, threw it on the makeshift table. Its strong cinnamon smell told them all exactly what it was. "A gift from him. I've brought plenty of squash from the garden as well." He held up the sack to indicate as much. They proceeded to get for him food and drink. Aggie walked behind him where he sat, catching a scent in her nostrils she did not care for.

"Here, May, help mother with the gourds. Derek and Gordon, you as well." Their mother, Sally Washbourne, had taken some preliminary steps to carve openings in the gourds. Now the children greedily worked at the task. Tonight, of course, all children would be in bed. But before then, there seemed no reason not to include them in the festival, for someday they, too, would march on Samhain Night to the clearing, to celebrate the New Year and perform the Rite.

Aggie rose up and began the story, same as she did every year, for the children must know what went before to preserve it for those who would come after. Her old eyes had begun seeing the shadows a few days earlier. Now the roaming, silent, gray figures stopped in their mysterious searchings. They left her alone mostly, except for one friend who spent each twilight of the past week in Aggie's rocking chair near her hearth. Aggie cleared her throat.

"Samhain, the Eve of Summer's End," she began, her thin voice cracking as the wind kicked up suddenly. "All goes down for the long frosty night. We are bereft of light, of warmth, yet we do not mourn their passing. We rejoice. They will come again.

"Look, if you will." Aggie pointed a bony finger toward the edge of the clearing where one particular shadow loitered. The children turned their heads, and she could see that one or two actually did observe the figure to which she pointed. Weylin looked up and around, seeing nothing but smiling politely. Aggie continued. "Departed friends traverse the Earth this night. This time of all the year, and this night in particular, is special. For tonight, the veil between the worlds is thinnest. Those who have come before return to visit. Likewise, this evening is the best of all possible times to visit the departed in the realms they now inhabit. But there is one more reason why this Samhain Night is special."

She paused a moment, drawing a breath, choosing to leave in place the stray gray hair that fell upon her face. She looked at them and past them as she spoke her next words.

"The Soul of Nature is a Green Man, my children; covered in leaves, skin like tree bark, horns on His head, hooves on His feet. Each breath He takes is mossy, leafy, musky. Each exhalation carries the smells of summer. Tonight is His final night upon this Earth. King He is of every leaf and branch and blade of grass. Of every animal that breathes and births and dies. Where He goes, they follow. When He is young, in Springtime, so too are His minions. When He dies, they follow loyally. Be not sad, for He will not wait long to see His Lady love. But His power on this Earth wanes and will not increase until Springtime.

He returns to Her dressed in His most magnificent costume, bearing gifts to woo Her. Now is the time to look
within, for on comes Winter. She will rule the Earth alone,
the ancient crone.

"Those who may follow the departed during the coming year harvest all they have learned to take with them,
coming around again to sow that which they did not learn
before. It is how all things here spend their time." As the
last sentence fell from her lips, she felt her power to inspire
to be unusually soft. The words were worn, their vividness
faded. Perhaps she had spoken them too often.

She watched two young girls strewing final necklaces
over the princely stuffed body of The Green Man. She
remembered it wasn't so long ago that these very girls were
the children, frightened of his fearsome eyes, carving
gourds, hearing her tale of Halloween. She sat down
wearily, looking up at the Green Man, and lightly ran her
finger over her chin.

It is said that hairs on the chin denote a Wise Woman.
Of hairs on her chin she had nine. Three for strength, three
for courage, three for sight. It was as her mother had spoken to her:

> *One and one, the dreaming's done;*
> *Two times two, the cards for you;*
> *Three times three, a witch you'll be;*
> *Four times four, meet at The Door;*
> *Five times five, from stars derive;*
> *Six times six, stir bones with sticks;*
> *Seven times seven, the guide to Heaven;*
> *Eight times eight, unlock The Gate;*
> *Nine times nine, at Her table dine;*
> *Ten times ten, Around Again.*

Three and three and three. A witch she'd be, and was. One of the few remaining. Agrippina Serafina Thumbelina Greenapple. Aggie, the Dawn Maiden, whose mother's mothers had advised Plantagenet kings, and well into the dark of remembered times guarded the sacred groves and wellsprings as Priestesses of the Old Ways.

Aggie of the Spiders, Aggie of the Willow, of the Meadow, of the Lucky Harvest, the Falling Coins and Flying Brooms, of any number of things, now ministered those Ways amongst any who would welcome them. She had, the last twenty or so winters, been settled with this goodly bunch, sought after as wise woman, healer—even teacher—yet always separate from their houses and lives, which made her mysterious, but gratefully anonymous.

Aggie, in Whom the Sight was Strong, could see that things were changing. A shade, not yet black, yet no longer gray, was gaining ground somewhere in the South, but how far South she did not know, and how long, how far, how deep it would go, she had only a shuddering notion. Far away as it was, it settled first in people's hearts, heeding no borders, creeping ever closer on little feet of fear and greed. There was great pain, but the shouts were ignored.

She kept her knowledge to herself; the innocent did not have much time left to their innocence.

Feeling unusually sad and weary, Aggie closed her eyes. A light breeze blew, and the Green Man's gaze shifted to look directly at her. His head inclined in her direction, his arms reached out, mouth bending in a garish smile that frightened her.

Suddenly he jumped from his pole and shambled towards her, shaky strides on stuffed straw legs, arms outstretched, gait as a puppet's. Aggie's mind bid her get up, to move, to flail her arms, but she could not will her body to be anything but still.

The pursuer halted as he reached her, stumbling forward, then began sinking into the ground, which now was a river of dirt. A sound came, high-pitched and shrill, that of air being sucked into the widening scar before her. The leaves covering his face and neck shook as he grasped at her, and he grinned as he sank into the dirt and the noise, arms lengthening to reach her, sewn eyes imploring her. Stick fingers pinched at her calves, trying for a hold, finding a skirt hem that would serve. The earth howled. Now he had an ankle and was disappearing fast into the gorge. The crone twisted, grabbing for hunks of grass that came uprooted in her hands. She slid along rocks and dirt to the lip of what was now a dark, unending pit. *Too late*, she thought. *If only I could concentrate.* She searched her memory for proper words, but the only thought that squeezed from her mind was a simple, *Away from me, it is my will.*

The stick fingers loosened, slid from her ankles, and disappeared down the shrieking pit, which promptly closed up. She could hear snarling, then knew it as the erratic rhythm of her own breathing. And then she was awake. Startled, she looked about and found herself surrounded by the others. Her heart pounded wildly as she tried to catch her breath. She realized she was no longer sitting, but lying on the grass. It appeared she had been screaming.

Fifteen minutes and several swigs of cider later she still drew deep breaths. The spirits grew thicker around them. She watched their ramblings dispassionately, feeling as though she had been slapped, the vision still resonating in her being. Shutting her eyes brought the intense fury of His eyes upon her. She avoided looking at the effigy, which hung on his post innocently, as before.

"Pardon me, mother Aggie, I was told you have the candles?" A smooth, low voice spoke behind her, causing her to jump. It was Weylin, the newcomer.

"I'm no one's mother. Not that you'd know anything of that. What other presumptions would you insult me with, stranger?"

Weylin regarded her patiently, then answered carefully, "Madam, I realize you've had a frightful episode, and it pains me to see you thus compromised. But there is no reason to be snappish. I've come for the candles. Do you have them?"

Aggie snatched up her pouch of alternating velvet, linen and leather, and reached inside for them. "They're right here…I put them here last night," she said, groping around for them in what seemed like bottomless blackness. "I remember quite well putting them here…Oh dear," she said, "where could they be?"

The soft lines of the youth's face hardened slightly. His eyes shifted down and up as he exhaled through his nostrils. "Well, that will do just fine," he said. "As if it weren't enough risk traveling here, now we'll be stumbling around in the dark. How will we see? What if we're recognized?"

Aggie rose, losing patience with this stranger. "You're a presumptuous one, you are. You think to hide it with your fine manners, your fine clothes. But you stink of lies. What you're doing here, I don't know."

"Well! I have not traveled this far—risked my safety—to be thusly insulted by the likes of you, spinster. I'll not walk without proper light. What if we are seen, all of us out there, as we truly are? Will they not question why we're out on this night, of all nights?"

"What if? What if? What if you go home right now and do not bother us with your complaints?" Aggie pointed a bent finger at him. "We do not have need of your fearfulness. We will walk by moonlight if we must," she continued. "As for risk, if you had fear of risk, young man, you wouldn't have come here to begin…"

All had ceased talking, and went about their preparations, keeping a wary eye.

"I think Weylin's right," said another voice. It was Justine, a woman whose gifts were strengthened by the fervent practice of her art. Aggie turned to her, fuming.

"You take his side, then? Never mind the moon hangs nearly full in the sky. You take the side of a stranger?"

"I take the side of good sense. You surprise me, Aggie. You'll bring a bad year upon us. You've had a fright, you're not yourself, but don't pick on this young man. He only has our good at heart." Aggie stared at Justine for a long moment, not believing she could conclude this foppish juvenile held good intentions toward anyone except himself. "You're tired, Aggie. Maybe you should sit down." All around her Aggie saw caring strangers, no longer her friends.

"I'll do no sitting while it's daylight. It's candles you want, it's candles you shall have. But heed my warning, there's no good'll come of that stranger. He stinks."

And with that she walked off.

Aggie walked a steady pace homeward, her stride now calmed to a purposeful walk, her anger easing, still stinging at the insults. She, the oldest they'd known in three lifetimes. She'd watched several born, marry, grow old, and die. Yet she lived on. She knew things they couldn't imagine; had conversed with creatures they would never guess existed. It was an insult, and a keen one. "They will no longer listen to an old woman, then let them make their own paths." With that she put them out of her mind, and turned her thoughts to other things.

Treading the familiar route, Aggie thought of Samhains past, of chanting the ancient songs.

Chanting the ancient songs.

Gathering in circles.

Spiraling to the center.

A never-ending dance.

She had made the invocations all her life. *To the North, to the South, the East, the West, to fire, water, air and earth. To the Goddess and the God. Join us, join us, on this most sacred Samhain night, when the veil between the worlds is thinnest and those that live beyond may roam freely throughout our world, as we through theirs. Those souls who will go through, now is your time. Close your eyes, my children. Close your eyes. What do you see?*

Aggie walked, eyes closed, her head cocked to one side, dwelling on the ceremony as it had been, picturing how it would be this evening, hiding from the thought that if she weren't there, others were who could take her place.

Looking up, she realized with dread that the moon was growing brighter and now hung as a luminous disk high in the sky, two days from full, smiling vacuously upon her. Blood moon, shining upon the night's thinning veil, marking the sacred passage of time, passing of lives; yet the moon returns and grows and thins and disappears again.

She took a few steps more, thinking how it was nearly dark, that she should have reached her home by now, that her mind had wandered. She lifted her skirt to hurry along, but stopped immediately, finding she stood at an unfamiliar crossroads.

Around her the spirits of the dead converged, now quite visible, ambling down one path or another, to and fro, a steady stream. This particular crossroads was a true crossing of paths: one straight this way, one straight the other. At the crossing's center lay a pile of stones a little more than waist high. Atop the stone mound sat a stone head of four faces, each pointed in its own direction. Two female, two male. It spoke out to her as she neared.

"You who approach for the first time, a cross is as good as a circle any time. Is a pond not as good as a river? A circle, once crossed, is no longer safe, but maybe a cross taken will encircle you. Know what we mean?"

She stood flustered for a minute, then: "What path do I take to get home? It's most important that I get home."

"That depends on where home is, does it not? Your home—hmmm, we see you have no home," replied the stone-faced oracle.

"I *do* have a home. I need to get the candles so I can get back by nightfall."

"Nightfall? Night's fallen. Day's crossed to darkness. You who have been here before should know that by now."

"Please! Just tell me how to get there."

"Now, now, don't get cross. You are given a choice. The path of return? The path of continuance?"

"Where will they take me?"

"That is for us to know and you to find out. One path takes you there, one path takes you here, one takes you somewhere else. You decide."

"What about the one I'm on?"

"Oh, you can't travel that again. It's already been gone over. Steps taken, tracked in the dust."

"You said I had a choice of continuance or return. What of that?"

The head fell silent.

Aggie walked around them, staring down each path, then at each totem guardian. She could read nothing from them.

She walked around again, closing her eyes, reaching down each pathway, allowing herself to open to the possibilities of each. Images leapt at her from each road.

"C'mon," said the head, "it's just a decision. So many to make in one lifetime. You'd think people would just get used to it. *Uch*, we know."

Aggie finished her circle, then, "I have no decision in this. There is only one path open to me. The others are unfinished shadows. Return and continuance are one and the same."

"Ooo, very good. And your decision is?"

"The candles, there's nothing to be done. I left them home."

"So be it."

Her pace slowed to a cautious walk, head turning from side to side, eyes glancing at every detail as she tried to recognize her new surroundings. Aggie wondered at the ancient forest of oak which she now trod, wishing silence from herself, to attract no attention amidst the vast, looming, rooted forest whose trees shone silver in the moonlight, whose arms twisted upward to a darkening, indigo sky, whose powerful presence overwhelmed her so she felt she might faint. Distant crickets could be heard, and the *crunch crunch crunch* of dead leaves wherever she placed a foot.

The wind kicked up, and on it she heard a faint melody, just enough to capture her attention. And when the wind died, so too died the song, leaving her bereft, longing to hear it again.

Just then the wind kicked up again, a little stronger this time, and the melody was back to soothe her. A trine of chimes, she thought, with no beginning and no end...such strange music, nothing to ground it. It's almost a wind blowing.... So strange, a chime that has no beginning and no end. What note is that, exactly?

With a delicate, slender hand, adorned with knobs and wrinkles, she pushed her graying hair behind an ear, lifted her head to the breeze, closed her eyes to listen, and walked after the notes. Her steps felt more like drifting continents—large, grand, deeply unsteady, relaxed and moving, as if she floated. Something glowed silver in the distance.

Her feet eventually led her to a stand of young trees, growing tightly together, a tangle of branches filling the spaces between their trunks, and no way to pass. Yet beyond their wall the silvery glow beckoned her. *The trees will part for me; they must,* she thought. "Won't you let me hear the music?" she asked.

"Who speaks?" A booming voice resonated everywhere around her, a unison of high, low and middle. Trees.

"It is I, Agrippina Serafina Thumbelina Greenapple, The Dawn Maiden, Aggie of the Spiders, of the Willow, the Meadow, the Lucky Harvest, the Falling Coins, the Flying Brooms and any number of titles bestowed on me by those to whom my gifts were magics. Won't you let me pass?"

"You are expected. Pass, but beware. Do not forsake the path."

The trees slowly shifted their branches. What seemed an impenetrable wall now provided a door just her height through which she passed with ease, watching the silver light loom up as she drew near.

At last she was at the music's source: a glimmering pond whose waters shone silver, whose voice had called her there and now sang to her in a thousand rippling chimes.

Aggie stepped into the clearing, humbled by its beauty. She knelt at the water's edge, gazing down into its luminescence. Gazing back at her were the faces of a thousand lifetimes, a thousand other selves, all familiar. "When was I looking for the fountain of youth? When did the fountain of youth reach out and find me?" she asked aloud. "Has this been here all this time and yet I have only found it now?" Tears streamed down her face.

"In a way," responded a voice so silken and deep it sent an unexpected shiver through her. "And yet you have always known Us. We have always been here. Since the beginning."

"As it has always been," said Aggie, standing to meet Him as He stepped near. He smelled of moss and roses. His breath was warm on her neck as He embraced her and she saw His face was a mournful one this night. Two ancient horns spiraled upward from His brow, the grand and intricate crown of the Old King.

"It has been a long, long time," she said.

"I have waited," He replied. "Come. Let me show you a place where all your follies have been triumphs."

Off came the black wool cape, the skirt, the shirt, the underclothes. Off came the dirty old skin of humans' making. Silly things. Now her nakedness matched His own.

He stooped and kissed her, then took her hand and they walked step by step into the pool. The chill filled the wrinkles and crevices of her body, until she was covered in the silky waters. She glided and drifted, and plunged her head under, letting the cold sensation rattle her brain as the water filled her ears. She opened her eyes and saw a sparkling whirlpool just below the surface, into which a multitude of souls went swirling.

Together they floated on their backs, watching the moon through the circle of treetops towering above them. How perfectly its shape mimicked the little pool which now held them suspended.

"I was afraid before. That's why I tried to run."

"Running only makes it worse," He answered from somewhere within His own experience. "Shall we go and see the One whose pool this really is?"

Aggie lingered for a long moment and then, drawing a final breath, submerged into the rippling waters and didn't come up again.

She floated. Floated through and over. Her roof, her garden. Someone would tend it...the path, the pathway gone awry...it no longer mattered.

And over there, the Stone Field. Justine had commenced with the ceremony, as Aggie knew she would. A kiss was needed to pass the chain along. Aggie swooped down to where the nine who would participate stood round the fire. She stood before Justine and placed an invisible kiss upon her forehead.

Then, with one swift blow they hacked him down, The Færie King, and with many blows thereafter cut him into pieces and buried him at the four corners. "Blessed be the coming year!" someone cried, and dancing commenced. Aggie stuck a pale gray hand into the Earth, digging out an apple.

"I'd best be going. See you all in Spring." And just then Justine looked over and nodded.

Aggie let herself float upward, somewhere hearing distant horses' hooves. "Run," she thought dreamily, quickly forgetting from what, as she floated toward a bright familiar light.

In the circle below, the dancers ceased just before six men on horses burst into the field. All tried to run for cover. All but Weylin, that is, who stayed behind to greet his friends.

Benjamin Gorman

Promise

Promise

by Benjamin Gorman

The waning days are once again at hand
(The mortal soul's reminder of its lot);
Through thin-necked glass drop precious grains
  of sand,
Each grain a day in Life's persistent plot.

At Autumn's close the winter winds bring Death
Who wanders, silent, 'neath the naked boughs;
His bony hands unwarmed by steamless breath,
His ears attuned to lovers' fateful vows.

The soul begins to wonder at its fate
In labored years 'twixt swaddling rags and shroud;
It blanches at the terrifying rate
That flesh decays and straightest backs are bowed.

This time of darkness holds for us a key:
The body's dissolution sets us free.

Joshua Mertz

Cold, Dark
and Waiting

from 1987 Sometimes the fun of Halloween is just saying ick! The next story, "Cold, Dark and Waiting," is a case in point.

Usually our writers wouldn't talk about their stories ahead of time (part of the fun was surprising everybody). But Joshua and I, as co-hosts, would typically bounce ideas off of each other throughout October. One year Joshua told me he was going to write a story about the gunk in the bottom of the refrigerator. We were both college bachelors at the time, so I knew exactly what he was talking about.

A few days later I came home to a long answering machine message—Joshua reading the middle part of his story, the long passage listing everything that ever went into the refrigerator and never came out. I knew immediately that this was going to be a great read-out-loud story.

"Cold, Dark and Waiting" is the oldest story in this book, and in terms of plot, perhaps the slightest as well, but every time I read that description it makes me laugh. As Joshua explains, "The fun of this story was coming up with every conceivable synonym for slime."

Cold, Dark and Waiting

by Joshua Mertz

It's dark in here. And cold. I lie, waiting, in the cold. The frigid darkness gives me time to think. I think about how hungry I am. I think about the light. I remember the light, back when I was somebody else. Now I am only hungry. Very hungry. And waiting for the light. Memories wash through me...

The house stands a ways off from the pavement, hidden by a dirty stand of unkempt pine. One reaches it by a twisting dirt road, having to cross a stony streambed before climbing a steep, rutted track to the abandoned front yard. Overgrown trees enfold the decrepit domicile like an insane mother bending over her stillborn child. Scant sunlight holds stunted roses at the brink of death.

The house had been put up by a share-cropper family near the turn of the century, but the father's religious convictions forbade medical "deviltry" and the entire clan expired of smallpox, scurvy and malnutrition.

In the Twenties and Thirties it became a hangout for bootleggers and was, for a few brief years, a lower-class brothel. Bullet holes still grace the walls.

Since then, a steady stream of shiftless, homeless, hopeless, nowhere people had inhabited the moldering wreck of a house. Beatniks and various itinerant messiahs stayed there, but only briefly, for the house was not felt to be conducive to true Zen. It is said that Jack Kerouac slept in the front yard one night, refusing to enter the ramshackle building because it reminded him of the ashes of his least favorite aunt.

The house was the scene of the grisly Formington Murders of the mid-Fifties wherein a hitchhiker tortured a family of five to death over a span of two weeks. An effort was made to raze the structure and put up a housing development, but the land was embroiled in complicated government escrow as well as having been deemed too rocky for profitable building. It became a spot for teenagers to take their trembling dates for some late-night groping.

In the Sixties, an idealistic band of hippies adopted the structure and dubbed it the "Love Ranch" (an ironic echoing of its days as a bordello). Halfhearted attempts were made to fix up the place, but the oppressive atmosphere surrounding the house, combined with a cornucopia of drugs, made for only neatly boarded-up windows and a few artfully painted mandalas. But before the dreams of better living through chemistry gave way to an unending quest for the all-powerful drug of money, the doomed commune tapped into the county electrics and ran a line to the house. They used the electricity to power a stereo.

And a refrigerator.

The refrigerator wasn't much: tufts of insulation poking through a cracked and stained plastic liner, a dim bulb dangling by two frayed wires, and a motor that made a sound like a wounded squid. Still, the miracle of compression and release followed immutable physical laws and the interior of the smudged steel box remained cool. Even, at times, cold.

Since its arrival at the house (August 12, 1965, at 7:32 in the evening), the refrigerator had never once been cleaned. The first food placed in the refrigerator, within minutes of its arrival, was a partial head of lettuce and the remains of a soybean and carrot casserole wrapped in waxed paper. These items were never removed. They were pushed to the back of the shelf by two six-packs of beer and a loaf of bread. There they lingered for many a month and became the seed elements of a complex and virulent organic soup that collected in the bottom of the insulated box over a period of more than two decades.

The house never stopped being a party location. The setup was simply too good for any group of hot-blooded, hard-living, born-to-be-wild youth to ignore. Remote, but not too remote, screened from the rural country road it faced, untended acres of field and woodland in which to play their glandular, alcoholic or hallucinogenic games, and, best of all, a working refrigerator.

The accumulation of rotting ooze at the bottom of the pitiful icebox grew in a fitful and random manner; a veritable stochasm of slop and slime. Spilled beers, mouldy beans, a wide variety of fruits and vegetables, much bread (mostly white), an occasional egg, a neglected bouquet of wildflowers, an assortment of greasy pizza pieces, a spilled jar of mayonnaise, quite a few soft drinks, an appreciable amount of wine, stale hamburgers and french fries, a lost and forgotten hit of LSD, some yogurt, a dead fish, and the contents of one partygoer's stomach, deposited one night in fabulous, gasping retches by a miserable personage on the brink of alcohol poisoning, are only a few of the rich panoply of organic substances that festered, molded, rotted and putrified at the bottom of the ancient refrigerator.

The seemingly patternless accumulation of carbon-based muck came to a turning point on a late winter night. Winds from a persistent storm managed to topple one of the sickly trees ringing the house. While not actually striking the structure, the tree managed to fall quite close to the house, rattling it to its soggy, wooden bones. Inside the refrigerator, the shock was sufficient to jar the dangling bulb free of its tenuous mooring and drop the live electrical wires into the disgusting mess lining the bottom.

Amid a shower of sparks and the smell of burnt rot, the wires shorted out. But not before they shot a tremendous burst of energy through the mouldy, gelatinous mass. Strange changes began to take place.

Scientists theorize that lightning bolts in some primordial soup back in the Earth's infancy gave rise to what later became life. A similar situation took place at the bottom of the dark refrigerator. Proto-nucleic changes swept through the slime, recombining and altering the organic material they came in contact with. The yogurt and the LSD—not to mention the decayed body of a rat thrown into the fridge many Halloweens past—played a seminal part in the redirection of the meta-synthesis taking place in the dark cold. The fetid goo achieved a level of proto-sentience. It became aware of its own existence. It became aware of its own feelings.

It felt hungry.

Kenny was a loser. Not that he ever lost a fight, or a drinking bout, or his heart to the flames of love; rather that he not only never amounted to much but had no intention of ever amounting to much.

He was twenty-seven years old and worked in a car wash. It kept him fed and sheltered and allowed him to maintain his battered Harley Davidson and indulge in several drugs. He had held the job for two years, a record. Kenny was an inveterate party animal. He was known to be a wild man who might do anything that came to mind when he was five or more sheets to the wind. Either the life or the death of a party.

Three pairs of Levis, two pairs of boots, a few T-shirts, and the remnants of several pairs of underwear were the sum total of Kenny's worldly possessions, excluding, of course, his motorcycle. The constant wetness of the car wash was the most bathing he had received in years. He was barely literate, mean-spirited, always fought dirty, and treated the rest of humanity with an acrid air of disdain and hatred.

He had had the name "Bunny" tattooed on his right arm one night in Atlanta when he was drunk, AWOL, and consorting with a floozie named, oddly enough, Bunny. Anyone who called him by that name was in for a violent surprise. Teeth had been lost and heads cracked over some facetious remark. Kenny had considered having it changed to something else, like "Punky" or "Bumpy," but feared that it might make matters worse. The only person who called Kenny "Bunny" was George Klump, leader of "Satan's Cuspidors," a local biker gang—whom the membership affectionately called "Punkin'." Other than George, Kenny respected no one.

Kenny's anti-social behavior did not bar him from all parties, only the tamer ones. Many a wild fling was staged out at the abandoned share-cropper's house in the country, and Kenny had more than a passing familiarity with the place.

So it was that he turned to the crumbling wreck of a house for sanctuary. The daughter of the owner of the car wash had not appreciated Kenny sticking his hand down her blouse when they were watching TV one evening, and George "Punkin'" Klump was in town looking to collect some money Kenny owed him. Good time to disappear for awhile. Halloween was a few days away, and a short hiatus from work, culminating with the inevitable wild bash sure to take place at the country house on Halloween weekend, sounded like just what Kenny needed.

He motored out to the abandoned farm in the cool of the evening, his backpack loaded with baloney, bread, and beer. On his long drive, Kenny thought fondly of having a cold beer whenever he damn well pleased for the next several days. And there is only one place to put beer to keep it cold.

In the refrigerator.

Kenny wrestled the unwieldy Harley up the rutted road, stopped in front of the house, and shut off the engine. A dusty silence fell upon the place. No birds sang, no soft wind nuzzled the trees; the only sound was the insectile ticking of the motorcycle's engine as it cooled.

Kenny stretched his sore muscles, grabbed his pack off the bike, and tromped into the house. When he opened the front door, rancid air washed out of the domicile, assailing his nose with the dusky smell of deep decay. He paid the effluvium little heed, for the house had always smelled bad, and put the odor down to some animal that had crawled under the house and died.

"Later for that," thought Kenny, for he really did enjoy the sight of mangled dead things. "Right now I need a beer."

He fished a cold can from his pack and popped it open, savoring the earthy, foaming liquid as he strolled through the house. Little had changed since his last visit: holes gaped in the walls, piles of dirt and debris crowded the corners, stupid hippie drawings were artfully inscribed with that most ubiquitous of Anglo-Saxon sexual expletives, and the ashes of a fire lay in the middle of the living room.

Kenny headed toward the kitchen.

He went to the refrigerator to stow his scant provisions. As he swung the icebox door open, a searing wave of putrid smell swept over him, causing his eyes to water and the skin on his arms to pucker.

"Screw it," the aging car washer thought. "In a little while I'll be too stoned to notice it."

Placing his bread, baloney, and beer on the topmost shelf, Kenny thought he saw the green slime at the bottom of the fridge move ever so slightly in a rippling motion. Passing it off as a trick of the light and residual hallucinogens, he helped himself to another beer.

The dewy can slipped from his partial grasp and landed in the glistening slime in the bottom of the box with a mucilaginous *schplopp*. Muttering curses, Kenny bent down and tried to fish out the errant beer by grasping the rim of the can between his thumb and forefinger. Much to his surprise, it would not budge.

Trying to keep his hand away from the reeking ooze, he braced the four fingers of his left hand on the rim of the can and pulled upwards. The beer can moved as if through partially fossilized Jell-O, but would not pull free of the foetor. A dripping tendril of slime lifted itself from the pond of goo and wrapped around the wet metal cylinder.

Kenny's eyes widened. He paused for a brief moment, trying to decide whether what he saw was real or not. Indecision has, through the ages, been the undoing of great endeavors. Kenny's momentary vacillation pushed him over the brink of Hell.

In the space of a heartbeat, a second string of slime, this one thicker than the last, had wrapped itself around Kenny's wrist. It burned like dry ice. With a cry, the illiterate outcast jerked his hand out of the refrigerator. The tendril stretched taut. It thickened rapidly under Kenny's terrified gaze then, like a long stringy strand of mucous pulled to arm's length from one's nose, drooped under the pull of gravity and plastered itself against the biker's body.

Kenny's fighting reflexes took over. His animal brain realized that it had to retreat from the pain. Flexing his knees slightly, he threw himself backwards, tearing free from the stinging rope. He landed on his back and immediately rolled into a fighting crouch. Fear and awe, emotions he denied having, washed through Kenny.

The refrigerator door was swinging shut, as it always did. A thick tentacle of ichor lifted from the bottom of the steel box and pushed the door open again. Kenny became aware of a burning on his chest, leg, and arm. The strings of putrid ooze had corroded through his clothing and were eating their way down into his flesh. He clawed and slapped at the fiery rivulets of slime. Glancing up, Kenny saw, or thought he saw, a forest of waving tentacles atop the puddle of guck in the bottom of the refrigerator, each disgusting palp opening and closing a small opening at its tip as if questing for air, or light, or food. The stench of the seemingly sentient putrescence hit Kenny like a cloud of tear gas. His stomach churned and a wave of dizziness passed over him.

Whether the frantic lone biker's next actions were inspired by a subliminal urge to save humanity from a fetid future, or were merely unthinking movement aimed at saving his own miserable carcass, will never be known. Kenny surged to his feet and was at the refrigerator in one stride, trying frantically to pull the door shut. He almost made it.

The door resisted mightily his attempts to close it. Kenny was lean and strong from his violent, reckless life, and the adrenaline coursing through his veins served only to amplify that strength. Yet the thick arm of green goo holding the door open resisted with the strength of a crazed animal. He managed to get the door to within two inches of closing. He braced his feet and leaned into the door with his shoulder. A moist vine of stinking slime shot out from the interior of the icebox and wrapped itself around Kenny's throat.

He leaned even more heavily against the door, hoping to slice this tendril from its parent body and contain the terror. Kenny watched in horror as the tentacle pulsated and rippled, growing thicker. The first wet burning touched his cheek and he abandoned the attempt to close the door, turning, instead, to flee. The door burst open, throwing him on his back. He struggled to his feet, ripping at the searing string on his face. Another rope of slime shot from the dark box and engulfed Kenny's right hand, pulling it free from his neck. The thrashing man looked at his hand and watched the flesh melt away from the bones, sucked down a throbbing tube of dripping filth into the metal maw of the refrigerator.

Emergency doses of endocrinal substances flooded Kenny's bloodstream and time slowed to a crawl. In slow motion he felt himself open his mouth to scream and noticed that the sound of his own screams of pain seemed to warble in a rhythmic fashion. Part of his mind watched in mute fascination as yet another stream of iridescent green putridity uncurled from the pool of rancid uhrschlcim and headed for his face, while another part of his mind tried to close his mouth in time. Too late.

The wad of rotten, reeking abomination hit him, like the obscene expectoration of some monstrous toad, square in the mouth, spilling its burning, choking, ungodly ichor down his throat. Dribbles of nauseating green oozed from his nose. The animal part of Kenny's brain, a well-developed area, directed his limbs to twitch and thrash and his hands to claw and tear at the snot-like ropes of feculent goo. His logical mind screamed at him not to inhale. In some far corner of his head, that part of the human mind that observes all events calmly watched as Kenny's tongue dissolved. His last coherent thought was that the world had turned green and that he was a beautiful plant, thirsting for the sun. The logical inner voice noted that he was seeing the world through a sheet of slime. His observer portion marveled at the exquisite pain of his eyeballs being eaten away by the pustulent muck.

At last, the struggling form that was Kenny twitched a few times, then lay still. The web of slimy, drooling strings that connected the corpse to the mess at the bottom of the fridge contracted, dragging Kenny's heavy body across the floor. That Kenny was still alive the proto-sentient putrescence had no doubt, for it could feel his screams of pain and horror throughout the loose gel of ribosomes that comprised its nervous system.

Kenny shrieked and gibbered in the dark corners of his mind. The pain would not stop. And now he felt the presence of the Invader, burning cold, taking over his body. Kenny's torture reached new heights.

In the kitchen of the dilapidated house, the slime-covered body of Kenny slowly got to its knees and crawled into the refrigerator, dissolving into the ever-enlarging pool of writhing mucilage even as he moved. Freed from its restraint, the refrigerator door swung slowly shut.

And so I wait. This new mind has broadened my horizons, showing me that there is a world out there for the taking. I understand the wonder of parthogenesis and look forward to the day when I can split into a thousand fragments and grow full and strong.

But first the door to this my birthplace and my prison must be opened. I am very hungry and it is dark and cold in here. Soon, though, soon. A celebration called "Halloween" is about to occur; a celebration, appropriately enough, of fear. Many people will come to the house. One of them will open the refrigerator door. I am waiting.

Steven V. Taylor

Organ Donors
in Nightmare Land

from
1990

One of my favorite sub-genres of horror is the story where all your sympathy goes to the monster. The bottom line is that humanity has always made it hard for evil creatures to distinguish themselves as evil, and it's getting harder every day.

"Organ Donors in Nightmare Land" is another story by Steve Taylor, and it's a particularly good read-aloud story: short, tight, funny and dead-on accurate. Also, as the name suggests, it's fairly, uh, wet...

So put on your galoshes and wade on in. After all, the monsters of the world can't help making big sticky messes. Heck, they're barely keeping up!

Enjoy!

Organ Donors in Nightmare Land

by Steven V. Taylor

Jeremy awoke to the dying screams of his little brother, Skippy. As Jeremy's eyes adjusted to the black October night, he focused on a creature hunched up in the middle of his bedroom. Standing about ten feet tall, the thing resembled a *Tyrannosaurus* in the early stages of decay. Leathery gray-green skin covered its body, though white bleached bone was exposed in some areas. Skippy, the source of all the racket, was impaled through the chest on the beast's three long claws, as the creature clinched the youngster in a grasp not unlike that used with a bowling ball.

The monster poked at the large meaty muscle of Skippy's thigh and said, "Hmmm, a little too rare for my taste..." With a squishy, crunching sound, he removed Skippy from his claw, picked him up again by the big toe, and held him out at arm's length. Taking a deep breath, the demon dinosaur exhaled a column of flame that completely engulfed the Skipster (as he was known around the playground). His Flintstone pajamas, though advertised as flame resistant, vaporized immediately, allowing the skin to bubble and eventually turn completely black. Satisfied his morsel was done to perfection, the pre-historic demon-thing turned off the gas and took the boy in both claws.

Jeremy watched from his bunk bed while the monster snapped his little brother's spine in the same manner a seafood lover cracks open a freshly cooked lobster. Savoring

149

the steamy smell of the entrails, the beast buried his face in Skippy's abdomen, dug around a little, and finally came up with the end of the intestine. The creature then pursed his rotting lips together and sucked down the boy's gut like a long spaghetti noodle, until the last few feet whipped around the beast's mouth and disappeared between his fangs.

Finally, the Mesozoic hell-spawn tossed the remains of his midnight snack into the air and caught it all in his mouth with practiced nonchalance. The muted crunching sound of the monster's chewing reminded Jeremy of Grape Nuts cereal. As the mutant dinosaur munched away on its boney morsel, it cocked its head to the side and stared at the ceiling with intense concentration. After a full minute of chewing, the creature swallowed hard, licked the residue off his fangs, and smacked his lips while continuing to contemplate the flavor. "August," he said. "Yup, definitely August." He smacked his lips a few more times. "August 17th...umm... 1984."

Thoroughly satisfied with himself, the beast sauntered up to Jeremy's bunk, taking interest in the child for the first time. With the blood of Skippy still covering his chin, the monster leaned over Jeremy until his face was only an inch from the boy's nose.

The thing paused a second for dramatic effect. Finally, in a voice so low it reminded Jeremy of the late night DJ on the local FM rock station, the murderous lizard said, "I bet I can guess your birthday."

Jeremy was unmoved. He blinked twice and let out a long, drawn-out yawn. The dinosaur-thing pulled his head back slightly, said "uh oh," and disappeared without fanfare. In the bunk bed below, the sound of Skippy's snoring reminded Jeremy that he would have a pain-in-the-ass tag-along on the way to school tomorrow, just like every day. Jeremy turned over in his bed.

"What a stupid dream," he said to no one in particular, and drifted off into a restful sleep.

Kronos, Lord Emperor of the Eternal Plane of Nightmares, Ruler of the Most Frightening Images in the Universe, Sculptor of All Subconscious Terror, was pissed beyond belief. "You are all a bunch of *wusses!!!*" he yelled at his monstrous minions. "You wimps are about as frightening as a field of dandelions!" Kronos sank back into his throne in a gesture of surrender.

"I just can't compete with Hollywood," he said with a sigh. "How am I supposed to come up with truly horrifying nightmares when Freddie Kruger is down there kickin' ass and getting screams. What I need is a couple of good Jasons...."

Kronos pulled out the 32-inch Sony Trinatron he'd stolen from the material plane last year. He remembered how easy it was to get the new television. All he had to do was enter the dreams of a Japanese TV salesman, pull out the guy's beating heart and show it to him. Kronos promised the salesman he would show him one of his own internal organs every night for the rest of his life unless he delivered a new television, a VCR, and a full library of horror films to the top of mount Fuji in one week. It was no problem. Adults still fell for the blood and guts thing, but those damn kids—they were becoming too desensitized.

Kronos popped *Hell Raiser II* into the VCR. His emotions ran somewhere between jealousy and respect as the screen played out one bone-crunching splatter scenario after another. In one scene, involving hypodermics and rotating blades, Kronos himself, master of all visions gruesome, averted his eyes from the screen, feeling squeamish and embarrassed. With one hand over his eyes and the other on a remote control, the horror master turned off the VCR.

"Damn, that's gross," he said to himself. "No wonder it's impossible to scare these kids." Kronos rubbed his face with the palms of his clawed hands, tired and frustrated. Slouched in his throne, he was almost ready to give up, while the television, no longer tuned to the VCR, played out some vapid Saturday morning programming from the material plane.

From the corner of his eye, Kronos watched the endless stream of stupid cartoons and innocuous commercials, when suddenly, it came to him. "That's it!" he yelled to his motley collection of semi-humanoid minions. "It's terrible! It's horrible!...It's *perfect!*"

Jeremy fell out of bed, screaming. He was beyond frightened, beyond panic. Instinctively, he made a mad dash to Mom and Dad's room, uncaring of the welcome he might receive at this time of night.

Jeremy's Mom, sensing an extra lump in the bed, pulled herself to consciousness. Turning back the blankets, she found her son in the fetal position, shaking like a Thanksgiving Jell-O mold.

"Jeremy," she said in her most motherly tone, "did you have a nightmare?" Jeremy nodded his head in an exaggerated gesture of the universal affirmative. "Would you like to tell me about it?" she asked, once again using her most reassuring mom-tone.

Jeremy tried desperately to squeeze the words past the tears. "It was horrible, Mom! It was terrible! I went to school and all the kids, Mom, all the kids were wearing Reeboks!"

Jeremy's Mom reached for the one sentence she used most when dealing with her son: "Jeremy, I don't understand..."

The young child looked up at his Mom with big teary doe eyes. "Mo-o-o-o-o-m!" he cried in frustration and fear. "I have *Adidas!!!*"

Somewhere on the eternal plane of nightmares, a god cackled mercilessly as his mutated servants stockpiled New Kids on the Block lunch boxes.

Susan Lambert

The Tree Who
Did Not Wish
to be Touched

from 1990

When is a story a Halloween story? There are certainly a lot of stock images that Halloween brings to mind: costumes and pumpkins and lurkers in the night. But what if a story doesn't have any of those?

Susan Lambert is a contributing editor to Boxoffice Magazine, as well as a documentary filmmaker and an accomplished screenwriter. She describes the origin of "The Tree Who Did Not Wish To Be Touched" this way:

> The morning of the Halloween party I was jogging through Griffith Park, mad at myself because I didn't have a story, and how can you go to a Halloween story party without a story? As I was stewing, I huffed past a lone tree that stood apart from the others and had high branches and I thought to myself, "Now that's a tree that does not want to be touched."
>
> That afternoon I sat down at my roommate's computer and pounded out this story, though I wasn't sure at first that I wanted to read it. It wasn't a ghost story or even particularly scary. In the end, though, I did read it, editing wantonly as I did so to perfect the tale.

What makes a story a Halloween story? A touch of death perhaps? A windblown leaf or two? The best criterion I can think of is that you know one when you see it. Have a look and decide for yourself.

The Tree Who Did Not Wish to be Touched

by Susan Lambert

Once, there was a tree who did not wish to be touched. It enjoyed being a tree, mind you. It just didn't like being handled by outsiders, by people. The tree lived in a large park with an abundance of trees that did not mind being touched—some even enjoyed it. Naturally, this caused the tree who did not wish to be touched much distress. The parkgoers, assuming this was a tree like any other tree, would lean against it, climb it, picnic under it, pull on its branches, sit on its roots, strip off its leaves and generally touch this tree who did not wish to be touched.

The tree did its best to keep its branches out of reach, to gnarl its roots into uncomfortable knots, to avoid giving shade whenever possible and to do its best to seem uninviting to the happy parkgoers. Usually it worked. Perhaps the tree actually looked unattractive to people or maybe somewhere deep down they actually sensed the tree's distress as they approached it—but whatever the reason, people almost never came close enough to touch. Until that fateful summer the neighborhood kickball team discovered what a perfect third base the tree made.

Oh, how the tree suffered. All summer long. Stomping and slapping and scuffling. All right there, all right on top of it. What a horrible fate. Shivers and moans. One gigantic kid—Franklin—would wipe his sweat off on the tree's leaves. It was depressing.

With autumn arriving, the tree figured upon some relief, desperate for respite. But no, every weekend and even some evenings, they'd be out there again. Its leaves turned red, then brown and when the tree shook with anger, it threw the leaves down at the boys. *Take that! Stay away! Don't touch me!* But its efforts failed it; the leaves were harmless to them. Featherlight and windswept, they rarely reached their target and never caused distress among the boys. Some of them even reveled in the darting leaves.

Then came the last day of autumn. A weekend, and the park was filled. People everywhere, picnicking and playing and struggling to relax on their last weekend before winter set in. The day was crisp and clear. And the boys were back. They brought their families with them. Loud, boisterous, happy families. More kids. More touching. Horrible.

A new boy joined the group. Leon, they called him—at least the parents, anyway. The other boys called him Limpy Leon, or Limabean Leon, because although he was a happy boy, a friendly boy, he just didn't like playing outside. He didn't like running and jumping and climbing and playing with other boys. He was the boy who did not wish to play.

Lunch came first and everyone ate. The tree was left alone. Leon was left alone. The tree wished hard and prayed to whatever forces trees might pray to. *Please, don't let them touch me. I do not wish to be touched. Please, no more.* The tree watched with horror as the boys came away from the picnic to start their game. Leon was shooed away by his parents and he stood aside as the boys chose sides. Finally, Franklin pushed him down and then picked him. He had to. Leon was the last one and Franklin had the last pick. Franklin wanted to just push him down and not pick him, but it was the last day of autumn, and the teams were uneven, and most of all, his mother was there.

Leon was pointed out to third base. The tree saw him coming and shivered inside its bark. *He's going to lean against me, pick at my bark, scrape my roots.* The tree braced itself for the touching. But it never came. Leon arrived at the tree, but did not lean, pick or scrape. He did not touch. He folded his arms and stood with his head down, next to the tree, without touching it. Close, but strangely unobtrusive. Leon did not want to be there. He did not wish to play. Both seemed to hold their breath for a moment. Leon lifted his head and stared at the tree, curious.

He has a soft face, thought the tree. Leon dropped his head.

The game began. With the excitement of the last game of the season, the boys quickly lost whatever interest they had in Leon. It was as if he wasn't there. Leon did not move, but slowly let out his silently held breath. He was going to be left alone. The tree, too, let out an imperceptible sigh. It was going to be left alone. The tree who did not wish to be touched had found the boy who did not wish to play and they were happy…

…Until the ball was kicked Leon's way. Franklin's team screamed for him to stop it. Leon stepped back, blinking a bit faster now, as the ball came flying toward him. Franklin was cursing now and running and saying something, but Leon stood deaf and dumb, his eyes locked on the ball speeding colorfully towards him. *Whooooooosh!* He and the tree watched it as it zoomed past. Leon took a hesitant, instinctive step for the ball as it headed for the street. The tree saw the car first and tried to warn the boy who did not wish to play.

"There's a car. Don't do it."

"I won't go after it," was Leon's answer, and it came before he even saw the car. So the boys stood and stared. Leon stood and stared. And the tree had no choice but to stand, so it also stared as the ball bounced off the curb, and gracefully bounded into the street and under the car. The car tried to stop, but squashed the ball quite easily under its tire. With a pop, the ball gave up its shape. The car rolled on.

A long, awkward pause followed. Before the storm. The the boys, led by Franklin, angrily turned on Leon. Leon just stood there, a bit stunned, as Franklin approached him in a rage. Parents were forgotten, decorum was out the window, Franklin was out for blood. It was his ball lying in the street.

Run, thought the tree to Leon, but Leon just stood there, wondering if he curled into a fetal position, would Franklin be too embarrassed to pummel him? Probably not.

The tree again cried out to Leon and Leon broke out of his trance, turned, and began to scramble up the tree. The tree trembled at his touch, but did not try to break away. In fact, it found itself helping the fumbling boy as he pulled himself up, branch by branch, away from Franklin and the boys who had now reached the bottom of the tree. Franklin screamed and yelled and jumped after him. But the boy who did not wish to play was indeed climbing the tree who did not wish to be touched. And doing a pretty good job of it. For, though it was a strain, the tree who did not wish to be touched was helping him, directing him, pushing him silently toward the strongest branches, the highest branches.

And then Franklin jumped up and grabbed a branch. The tree shuddered and Leon almost lost his grip with the movement. The tree screamed and shivered and tried to wrest its branch from Franklin's grip, but Franklin swung himself up and followed after Leon. Touching and climbing and prying and reaching for Leon, who had reached the highest point and sat, miserable, among the leaves. It was only a matter of time, as Franklin scrambled closer to him.

The boys below egged him on. They cheered and slapped the tree and started to reach for the branches themselves.

The tree was in agony—this had to stop. It struggled to get away. To get away from evil hands that touched. It had to get away. The tree pulled and strained and struggled and lunged to get away from the Franklin boy and, finally...

Leon felt the tree jump just as Franklin was almost upon him. He held tight as the tree tottered and fell. Franklin yelled and the boys screamed and ran out of the way. Leon just shut his eyes and held on.

The tree wobbled and then toppled over, pulling up its roots from the earth. It slammed into the ground with a mighty crash, shuddered once, and was still.

Leon stumbled away from the branches and looked up to see the parents running toward him. He brushed off the leaves from his shirt. The boys stood still behind him, stunned into silence. Until one boy said quietly, "you've killed him." Leon turned to shut him up. He was sorry about the tree, but it wasn't his fault. He'd felt the tree pull itself out of the ground, amazing as it had seemed. He didn't do anything to the tree. If anything, it was Franklin's fault. He started to snap back at the boy when his eyes fell on Franklin: his body caught underneath the tree, his face poking out between the branches, his eyes frozen wide. The side of his head resembling the deflated ball that lay in the street just a few feet away.

Leon heard the parents running up behind him. He felt the commotion and the hatred of the boys swirl around him. He started to sway on his feet; he needed something to hang onto, something to keep him standing. He reached next to him and touched the tree.

Michael Mayhew

Graveyard

from
1995
Nineteen ninety-five was the tenth year of our annual ghost story party, and something was nagging at me—we had almost no ghost stories. Vampires? Plenty. Zombies? Galore. Jack-o'-lanterns that come to life and wreak havoc? Hundreds! But a simple, "Why, son, the girl was murdered in this very room, and now sometimes, on foggy nights..." None. Nobody wrote about ghosts for some reason. So I decided to give the genre a try.

But there was something else. I'd become fascinated with El Día de los Muertos—*The Day of the Dead*—the Mexican holiday that takes place just two days after Halloween, but which seems to have such a different attitude. Both holidays ritualize death. But while Halloween fears it, The Day of the Dead embraces death as part of the natural cycle of things. The Mexican holiday combines a Thanksgiving style family gathering with an almost Asian ancestor worship. I began to wonder if the traditions might be induced to dance together. I sat down to begin my holiday-fusing ghost story.

But, as usual, something else happened along the way, and the story became its own thing. I'm still not sure we ever got a true ghost story. But I'm very happy with "Graveyard."

Graveyard

by Michael Mayhew

"Dad, come look! A graveyard!"

That was Paul. Paul is ten. He is my son.

I was at the desk in my father's study, in my father's house, miles from the nearest graveyard—at least geographically. Emotionally...well, we'd only buried Pops a couple of weeks before. Now I was sorting through a stack of lawyer's papers. It was more than a weekend's work, but I wanted it to be over with as soon as possible. Pops had taken his own lingering time to go. Mom had divorced him and moved to the Ridgecrest Retirement Center while he was still in the hospital, and I was left to clean up the mess.

"Dad, hurry! A graveyard!" Paul tore into the room in muddy shoes and a Spiderman tee shirt.

"Jesus, Paul! Watch the carpet." Paul looked chagrined, and stared down at his feet, as if he'd just realized he had them.

"Uh oh..." He turned to go back outside.

"No! Freeze!" He froze. I got up and lifted him. "If you walk back outside you'll make more footprints."

"I could walk on top of the old footprints," he suggested.

"Thanks, but no thanks." I carried him outside and set him on the back porch. As soon as he was on his feet he was tugging at my arm. "Let's go, Dad! Come look! A graveyard!"

My son is a macabre child. He loves bones and tomb-
stones. Burying Pops was like Disneyland to him. Not that
he enjoys seeing people suffer. If anything, he is too empa-
thetic. No, it's the actually *being dead* that absorbs him. He
can spend hours looking at a dead baby bird. He loves to
give himself the shivers. If he hears that someone has died
he wants to know all the details. If he already knows all the
details then he wants to share them. And then, in October,
there are the altars. When I was a boy, I built model air-
planes. Paul makes altars for the dead.

Used to be, Halloween was the first event in the holiday triple-header. You woke up on November first and
knew that you had to nurse your candy three weeks until
Thanksgiving. For my son, Halloween is the face of a coin
whose obverse is the Day of the Dead. Most of our neighbors are Hispanic, and all up and down our block, people
were preparing altars of food, candles, and *papier mâché*
skeletons—leaving front doors open for the returning spirits of their ancestors. Paul loves this time above all others. It
would not be exaggerating to say that he is obsessed with it.

By mid-October our house is filled with altars: altars for
my grandparents, altars for the turtles, newts and hamsters
Paul has had as pets, and an altar for Paul's mother.

Her death, many years ago, is obviously at the root of
all this. I've had a couple of child shrinks explain that to me.
As if I couldn't figure it out for myself. What they couldn't
agree on is what to do about it. One said Paul's altars were
harmless, the other said that they were a sign of deep problems. For myself, I do not know. I don't understand my
son. If Bonnie were around maybe she could help. Paul
reminds me in many ways of her. But she's not. Paul's opin-
ions notwithstanding, dead is dead.

Around the side of my parents' house is a place where nothing grows. When I was a kid we had a sandbox there, but after a few rainy winters the sand mixed with the clay soil and formed a sort of concrete, which was too tough to play in and in which nothing, not even weeds, could grow. When my father died I asked the gardener to till in some compost and try to grow something, anything, that might make the spot a little prettier, and the house a little more salable.

This is where my son led me.

About a quarter of the plot was rototilled in two-foot-wide swaths up and back. The tiller was parked halfway down a return run, and next to it was a battered yellow Tonka dump truck, its bed in several shards where the tiller had hit it. The gardener was digging nearby. Just as I came around the corner he pulled out a plastic *Triceratops*, caked in clay and strangely familiar.

"See Dad," said Paul, both scared and tickled to death, "the Graveyard of Toys."

The gardener pulled another dinosaur out of the earth. What was the guy's name, Pedro? Carlos? Pops would've called him José and left it at that. Pops called all Hispanic people José.

"I don't think it's exactly a graveyard, Paul," I said. But while I could say what it wasn't, I couldn't offer any explanations as to what it was.

Carlos, or Pedro, who at this moment looked more like John Marsh, the eighteenth century paleontologist, methodically pried out more toys. Now a mud-covered robot, next a Starship *Enterprise* in four pieces. Finally, a vaguely doll-shaped mud ball. I picked it up and got the shivers myself, like someone cold and close by was watching. I knocked the clay off its face and wiped it clean as best I could...and felt even colder.

"These are my toys," I said.

The day my father died I was with Paul at a birthday party for one of the neighborhood kids. Pops had been sick for almost a year with a cancer that had started in his liver and worked its way out. I knew he was gonna go soon but I had promised to help with the party so there I was. I remember very distinctly being out in this nice backyard, surrounded by screaming kids, and noticing my son standing alone, like the eye of a storm, nodding his head and listening.

I went over to him, to see if anything was wrong, and he turned to me with a faraway look and said, "Grandpa says goodbye. He says he doesn't hurt anymore. He says he's sorry."

That was maybe ten minutes after one in the afternoon. My father had died at One P.M. exactly.

I don't know why I suddenly remembered that.

About an hour after we found the toys, my mother called.

"I'm working on your databank," she said. Over the wires I could hear the strange crunchy/squeaky noise that she makes the phone make when she's gone lunatic. I often try to visualize how she must be holding the phone to make it do that, but I can never quite manage.

"My what, Mom?"

"Your databank. The data in your brain. I'm gathering the information that you need. You're very naive, Jason. The companions will be calling your boss and your doctor and your neighbors. You have to tell them that there's no history of schizophrenia in our family. That's genetic, you know. You don't want anyone trying to contaminate Paul. Your father says so, too."

"Pops is dead, Mom."

"Your father is a cocksucker!"

"That may be so, but he's a dead cocksucker." I checked my watch. A few years ago I decided that five minutes of paranoid delusion is what I owe my mother on any given afternoon for having brought me into the world. After that, any way out of the conversation, including abruptly hanging up, is fair game.

"You need me to help you, Jason. That's what family meetings are for. We'll have a family meeting when your father gets back…"

I set the phone down on the table while my mother rattled on obliviously. Had I told her I was going to be at the old house this weekend? I didn't think so. Mom has that creepy intuition that really crazy people sometimes have. Never useful enough to win the lottery or anything, but still…

My mind drifted into options mode. There was no way to counteract the dozen or so false assumptions upon which her monologue was built. That left switching topics or bailing out. Bailing out was looking real good. But there was something…

I picked up the phone. "Mom…? Mom? Mom!" She paused. "Mom, I found Billy Bear today." Silence on the other end of the line. "Mom, he was buried in the old sandbox."

"I gave you Billy Bear when you were three…"

"Yeah—Mom? Did you bury a bunch of my old toys by the side of the house? Or maybe Pops did it?"

There was a long beat. Then…"The companions! They're monitoring you for emotional stress!"

I hung up.

One time a couple of years ago, when Mom had first moved to Ridgecrest, I took Paul to visit her there. She'd been pretty well behaved, really. I mean, for her. But as we were walking out to the car Paul turned to me and said, "Who are the men that follow Grandma?"

"What men?" I said. We'd been alone with her in her room the whole visit.

"The two men who talk to her. They're mean. One of them yells at her and the other one whispers into her ear..."

The next three hours I spent back in the study, working my way through will and escrow papers and my father's affairs. At dusk I got up to find Paul and fix some dinner.

I found him in the living room, building an altar out of the toys. He'd arranged the toys from biggest to smallest on the coffee table, surrounded by piles of Ritz Crackers and Fig Newtons, and somehow he'd dug up a bunch of candles and set them ablaze amongst the toys. Puddled wax, crumbs, and mud were everywhere.

"Paul, what are you doing?!"

"It's an altar for the dead children."

"Paul, we don't *have* any dead children in our family. Look at this place! People are coming to see the house tomorrow." Paul got that 'morning after the night before' look he does so well, and then tried the old blame hand-off.

"But Hector said..."

"Never mind Hector!" Hector is a boy in our neighborhood back home—Paul's Day of the Dead guru.

"Paul, you've broken so many rules I don't know how to list them. But the biggest one is *never* play with fire. What would have happened if you'd burned the house down?"

He looked at his toes. "But, Dad, if we don't make an altar, the spirits of the dead will walk around the graveyard crying all night."

"If you don't jump into the tub this minute, you'll be the one crying all night."

Paul sulked into the tub, scowled through dinner, and whined into bed. It was strange—before they divorced, my parents had turned my old room into a "guest room." They never had any guests, but there was a bed there. I found myself tucking my son into bed in my old room.

"Dad," said my son, "will someone light the candles on Mom's altar tonight?"

"We'll do it tomorrow night, Paul." He looked troubled, but he was through complaining. I tucked him in and kissed him goodnight, and then, as I was closing the door, Paul said a funny thing.

"Be careful, Daddy. Someone is watching you."

What do you say to that? I promised to be careful and closed the door.

The cleanup took about two hours. I blew out the candles and threw away the crackers, scraped off the wax, Spray-n-Vac'd the carpet and ate the fig Newtons. In the end, I was left with a bunch of broken toys. They really were useless. Even old Billy Bear reeked of mildew. Suddenly I felt old and tired. I felt like I had fallen asleep watching the story of my life and missed most of it. What had I done with my life besides work every day? I couldn't remember. Finally, I took old Billy Bear outside and threw him in the trash.

The night was damp, but starry. A low fog hung a foot or so above the ground and swirled around my feet as I walked. An evening to fit my dark mood. I wandered through my parents' yard—looking out on the hills and fields where I was sure I must have played once, though I could not recall it.

Then I heard something. A soft scrape of metal. A quiet grunt. I followed the sound around the side of the house, toward Paul's Graveyard of Toys. Another scrape. Gravel and steel. And another sound. Sobbing.

I rounded the corner and then stood frozen. The fog was thickest here. It seemed to be oozing out of the ground itself. The air was very cold. But that wasn't what had stopped me.

A small boy was in the middle of it all. A boy with a shovel.

"Paul...?"

The boy didn't answer. He just kept digging. And weeping. In any case, it wasn't Paul. Paul has dark features and this boy was fair. They might have been cousins, though.

Tears streamed down the boy's face. His nose was running. He never stopped working.

"Hey..." I took a step closer, "what's wrong?"

The boy looked up at me for the first time. When he saw me his face contorted with rage. "Liar!" he said. "You promised!" Then he ran.

"Promised what?!" I took two quick steps after him. "Wait!"

On the other side of the tilled plot there is a gate. I found it locked with a rusty padlock. The boy must have climbed the fence. I wondered if I should try to follow. Was that a neighborhood kid? What was he doing digging up my parents' yard? Who did he think I was?

Thinking about it, for some reason, made me very edgy. A breeze stirred the fog, like lazy cream in a coffee cup, raising goosebumps on the back of my neck. Suddenly all I wanted was to run back inside. I made myself walk.

That was a mistake.

The back door was open.

All the doors were open.

Inside the house there were muddy footprints. A child's footprints. Everywhere. They ran up and back each hallway, ran in concentric circles in the living room, over the couch and the coffee table, on the walls. On the ceiling. The house stank of fresh damp loam. It would be impossible to clean. The mess was everywhere. All places. Ubiquitous.

Then it hit me. The guest room. My old room. Paul!

I tore down the hall in a burst of adrenaline. The doorknob was covered in damp earth. Opened the door. Mud everywhere. But Paul...Paul, a nice reassuring lump under the covers, I ran over and pulled them back and...

Toys. Dinosaurs. Broken model spaceships. Smell of mildew. Billy Bear where Paul's head should have been. No Paul. No son. You just can't hang onto anyone in your family, can you?

"Paul!" No answer. "Paul!!" Back into the hallway, into the study, all the lawyer's papers had been thrown onto the floor. Fog poured in through the open window like a slow-motion waterfall. "Paul!" No. Silence. Lost. Gone.

Down the hall. Empty.

Through the kitchen. Gone.

Past the living room. Lost.

Beyond the living room there was a doorway.

My parent's bedroom...I reached for the door...and hesitated...

I realized that I had avoided this room the entire weekend. I'd even planned on sleeping on the couch in the living room.

I also realized another thing. The muddy footprints had not crossed this threshold. Whoever had stolen my son and fouled the house I grew up in—making sure to miss no spot—had avoided this room.

I tried the door. Unlocked.

I went inside.

The room had a grey-blue quality, cold, austere. Nothing had been touched. Faded brocade comforter on the bed. Walnut surfaced dresser with a thin layer of dust on top. Framed photo of Mom and Pops, taken just before she left him. Two forced smiles. It was all as my father had left it.

No, as my mother had left it. Pops hadn't changed a thing. I don't know why but I suddenly felt like the room itself had given him cancer. The life they had made had poisoned the air. The bluish light cold as a glacier.

"Paul?" My voice way too loud and shaky sounding in this tomb. Some rooms have live walls, echoey walls. This one sucked up my voice and gave nothing back.

"Paul?" I flicked on the light—garish, too bright. Made myself look under the bed. Dust settling. Opened my father's closet—there were his suits and jackets. His golf clubs that he never used.

"Paul?" I tried the other closet. My mother's closet. Empty. Empty except for this: spaced at perfect intervals of maybe a centimeter were eighty or so lime green wire coat hangers. They waved ever so slightly as if underwater, periodically tapping each other with an almost silent *ting*.

The phone rang. I ran to it— "Paul, is it you? Are you okay?"

"What are you doing in my bedroom, Jason? I didn't say you could go into my bedroom. Are you spying on me, you little sneak? You little shit? Reporting back to your masters? You always were a sneaky little boy..."

"Mom..."

"A dirty little boy..."

"Mom..."

"A filthy, sneaky…"

"Mom, shut the fuck up!"

Amazingly, she shut up.

"Mom, I have to go, I'm doing something important…"

"You can't find Paul, you know…"

"What about Paul?"

"He's gone over to the other side."

"What? What are you saying?"

"I know when you've been up to your mischief, Jason!
A mother has certain instincts! And you've been spying,
spying, spying!"

I hung up. Jesus! How does she do that? *Why* does she
do that? I needed help. Who could help? I picked up the
phone again. Dialed 911. And felt…*guilty*. I realized that
the single greatest feeling I had about 911 was not that it
was the emergency number, but rather that it wasn't for me
to use. *It's not a game, Jason.* That's what I remember being
taught.

Is that what this night was? A game?

"Emergency," said a woman's voice.

"Yes, I uh…I…"

"Yes..?"

Why couldn't I say what was wrong? Because so much
was wrong? Can you call 911 and say, "my mother is a mali-
cious schizophrenic and she makes me feel like a frightened
child?" Can you call 911 and say, "I feel utterly alone, and
as near as I can tell I've always felt that way?" Can you call
911 and say, "the person I love most in the entire world has
gone away and I didn't even know how I felt until I lost
him?" No, just the facts.

"My son is missing. I can't find him."

"How long has he been missing?"

I checked my watch. "Ten minutes...maybe fifteen... I know that doesn't sound like very long at all but..."

"Stay calm," she said, "he can't have gone far."

Oh, lady, you don't know. The fog was in the house now, oozing into my parents' bedroom from the hallway, tracing hoarfrost patterns onto the bedroom window. Patterns of faces peering in—gape-mouthed, dead-eyed faces watching me, waiting for my next move. *Oh, lady, I should not have called. 911 is for fires and heart attacks.* Across the room from me, wire coat hangers undulated in a secret breeze. A dirty boy. *Ting.* A filthy boy. *Ting.* Coat hangers tapping. What do we do to dirty boys? Oh Jesus...

"Sir? Sir, would you like me to send a police officer?"

Without answering, I put the phone down on the cradle. Went back to my mother's closet. Traced an index finger along a wire hanger. Cold. Burning cold. What a mistake to come here. What a mistake to try to clean up this mess.

What do we do with dirty boys? We make them take their clothes off and we stand them in a corner...

With filthy boys...?

...and we take a clean wire hanger from the closet and we hold it before them so that they can watch as we...

With boys who make messes...?

...casually, grinning, unbend the wire until it is a single, three-foot length with a nice hook for a handle and we...

With boys who forget to *clean their room!*

...beat them until they bleed, until they are covered with welts, until they beg and scream and cry and promise never never never to do it again.

That's what we do.

Oh Jesus.

The fog parted before me as I walked out into the garage. I had a fragment of a plan. A half of a hunch. A whisper of an instinct. I wanted so badly to run outside, to hunt in the fog with a flashlight, to wake the neighbors. I wanted to do that more than anything, and I knew with absolute certainty that if I did that then when the sun came up Paul would be gone forever, dissipating with the mists in the hard clearheaded light of the morning. Something inside was saying: look in the places that frighten you...

Say what you will about him, Pops had great tools. I took the one I wanted from a hook on the wall and went back inside, mist parting in front of me like theater curtains.

I took the first coat hanger from her closet. *Snip*. Cut it with the wire cutters. *Snap*. An inch-long piece of wire fell to the floor. *Snip*. Another segment. *Snap*. And another.... In thirty seconds the hanger was a scattering of wire bits on the floor. Eighty more to go. *Snip*. *Snap*. Each segment brought another memory. *Snip*. The beating for coming home late. *Snap*. The beating for using dirty words. *Snip*. The beating for not cleaning my plate. *Snap*...

Time crawled naked on a field of broken glass. I was wasting time. I was losing Paul. I was tormenting myself for nothing. *Snip*. The weekend locked in my room with only water. *Snap*. The time I came home with a girl from school and Mom paraded around the living room naked, screaming obscenities...

It took almost an hour. By the end my hand was cramped and swollen. My jaw ached from grinding my teeth. But finally I found the fair-haired boy. The child in the fog. The thief in the night who had stolen my son.

I remembered the night Mom threw Billy Bear away.

'You're too old for a teddy bear.'

'No, Mom, no!'

'You're not a baby, are you?'

'Mom, please don't throw him away. I'll keep my room really clean. I'll put him in the closet so no one will see him!'

'Baby! Baby! Jason is a baby!'

Later that night when she had gone to sleep, I stole outside and dug him out of the trash. I put all my other favorite toys in a box and took them outside and buried them in the sandbox so that she couldn't take them away.

And I promised myself that when I was big enough I would dig them all back up and take them someplace safe with me.

After that, I never had toys again.

After that, my room was always clean.

I sat on the corner of my parents' bed, staring at an ocean of wire snippets on the floor, my memory foul and reeking with my own dark past. And for what? I had found the thief and it didn't matter. I still couldn't stop him. I still had no clues as to where he had taken Paul.

A voice in my head was saying, *Nice job, you've wasted an hour that you could have spent finding Paul, in here feeling sorry for yourself. What a terrific father you are.*

Without thinking, I knelt on the carpet and began picking up the pieces of wire, tidying, tidying, always tidying...and I caught myself. As I stood up I caught my reflection in the mirror—the cowed stoop of my own posture, the beaten look in my own eyes. Behind me, reflected in the glass, were the shifting frost faces of the watchers. Souls of the dead children. Watching and waiting...

I wanted to cry. I felt sick. Before I could run to the bathroom, before I could even think at all a great heave of bile rushed up my throat and spattered onto the carpet in a reeking puddle. I began to sob, gasping for breath. Tears streamed down my face and I was still heaving. I staggered backward, sobbing, moaning—*wanting more than anything to find a towel and clean the carpet!* My stomach was knotted and my sight was bleary with tears and my mouth was burning and my son was lost and I wanted to clean the fucking carpet!

"No!" I threw the wire across the room. "I am through cleaning everything up!" I yanked the drawers from the dresser and threw them at the wall. Gouging it. Breaking drawers. Scattering socks and neckties. "I am sick of waiting for it to be my turn!" I grabbed the mirror from the wall and smashed it into a thousand shards. I tipped the dresser over and kicked it until the wood cracked. I grabbed all of Pop's suits from the closet and tossed them on the floor and jumped on them.

"Where were you when she was beating the crap out of me!" I took the golf clubs and charged the faces in the window, the bloodless watchers, and threw the clubs through the glass—shattering it.

I ran outside into the fog and paced until I found some mud and I did the twist, coating my shoes, and ran back into my parents' bedroom and jumped on the bed with both feet—ruining the comforter.

"This is what you get. This is what you get. This is what you get. This..."

...was kinda fun. Bouncing up and down like a man on the moon, keeping a nervous eye on the ceiling so as not to hit it, and...*making a big damned mess...*was fun. The voice in my head tried to ask how this was gonna help find Paul.

"Shut up, Mom," I said, and bounced a little harder.

Outside, a breeze stirred the fog into eddies and swirls. I thought I saw more faces there, but I tried not to think about them. I just kept jumping.

I jumped on the pillows. I jumped on the comforter. I kicked it off the bed and ground it into the mess I'd made on the floor. Then I jumped back onto the bed to destroy the clean white sheets and started to bounce and heard something.

Something outside.

Something in the fog.

Something merry.

Laughter.

Outside in the fog there was laughter. A boy's laughter—no, two boys, laughing and out of breath. In the night. In the dark. In the fog.

I stepped off the bed, *gently.* Whatever was happening I didn't want to break it. It is a game, I thought. Tonight is a game.

I eased through the shattered window out into the fog. Damp dead faces swirled all around me, brushing against my face and arms. But ahead there was laughter. Suddenly a shriek, then a squeal.

"You're *it!*" screamed a boy's voice. Paul's voice! Paul was here. Then suddenly there he was, barreling out of the mists and right past me, disappearing again into grey eddies.

I shouted for him "Paul! Wait!" But he was long gone, laughing into the November night. I turned to chase him, catch him, carry him home—and the fog cleared. It didn't go away. I couldn't see the house or the hills, but I had stepped into a hole in the fog, a bubble of clarity inside the fog about the size of a room. It was colder here. Freezing. Cold like when I had recognized Billy Bear. Cold like when I had first seen the fair-haired boy. I knew this cold. I turned around again.

There he was, standing at the edge of the fog, ready to bolt into the grey, watching me warily. I started to move toward him, to shorten the space, but he tensed, edged away, half-swallowed now in mists.

"Wait..." I said, quietly now, "don't take Paul away. Please don't." I began to move closer again, very gently. He saw what I was up to but he let me. "I know how you feel," I said, "and I know what you want...but Paul deserves a childhood, too. Don't take him away."

I was just two feet away now. The boy studied me with a serious expression. Then he jumped. Not backwards—forwards! He slammed my chest with a tiny, ice cold hand and shouted "You're it!" Then he bolted into the fog. I raced after him.

That's what it came down to—chasing the ghost of my childhood through a sea of confusion. Zig-zagging through fog, following a trail of laughter, chasing my own tail, tripping, stumbling, swearing, picking myself up and dashing forward again, all over the yard where I grew up but had never played.

Night was lifting when I finally caught him—cornered him where fence met fence. He turned—dodged one way, I blocked him—dodged the other—blocked again.

"It's over, kid," I said. "I win."

The boy backed himself all the way into the corner, and froze—eyes glassy.

He's terrified, I thought. Then, *of course he is.*

"Hey," I said, "I'm not Mom. I'm not gonna hit you."

"Aren't you mad?"

"No. I was. But I'm not." Silent tears started to stream down his cheeks.

"I need to take Paul back," I said, "and I need to take you back."

He stood frozen, crying.

"Please..." I said.

He sniffled. Wiped his nose on his shirt. Reappraised me.

"Will you take Billy Bear?"

"Yes."

"Will you take my dinosaurs?"

"Yes."

"Will you take my Starship *Enterprise*?"

"Yes."

"It's broken, you know, you'll have to fix it."

"I know." The fog was beginning to glow orange with the dawn, beginning to burn away. "I've missed you, Jason. Come back home."

And then he walked simply and directly into my arms, and I lifted him up.

"It's warmer here," he said. "I've been very cold."

When the first stab of direct sunlight pierced the fog he dissolved away. Into my arms. Into me.

The mist was lifting. The birds were singing. I could see the entire yard.

I still had no son. I quickly scanned the yard. He had to be here. Had to be! Panic rising. Direct warm light on the grass. A hundred footprints in the dew. I'd lost him! I'd failed him!

For the final time that night, I remembered. Remembered words I didn't even know I knew—"Ollie Ollie Oxen—Free Free Free!"

Paul stepped out from behind an oleander bush.

I had to smile.

The house was a disaster and I didn't care.

"That kid was fun, huh, Dad?"

"Yeah, he was a good kid."

"Do you think he'll want to come play again?"

"I think he'll want to play a lot."

Paul appraised the living room. "We have to clean this, don't we, Dad?"

"Yes, we do. We'll do it together."

"Can we get breakfast first?"

"Sure..." I turned to walk him toward the car, but there was one final thing. "Paul... can you show me how to make one of those altars you make?"

He turned to me, grinning, and nodded. "You want to make an altar for the souls of the dead children?"

"Something like that," I said. I'd explain better later. Right now I wanted some pancakes, and to get back to my own home. There would be plenty of time later to build a shrine.

For the children with dead souls.

Joshua Hicken

Autumn

from
1995

Joshua Hicken was the youngest attendee at the Halloween story parties. The son of one of the 'regulars,' Joshua had heard about the parties for years from his father, and when he learned that we were going to retire the event after the tenth year, he insisted on being allowed to go to that final blowout. After thinking about it, we decided to bend our usual "adults only" rule (he really is a very bright and special kid).

When Joshua read this poem at the 1995 party, the innocence and simplicity of it struck a chord with all us jaded grown-ups, and we offer it here in that same spirit.

Autumn

by Joshua Hicken

Scary, Foggy
Leering, scaring, blowing
Pumpkins growing quickly
A time for scaring
A time for carving
It's getting very windy
Pumpkins leering
Trees are getting bare
Fall

Joshua Mertz

The Demon's Wish

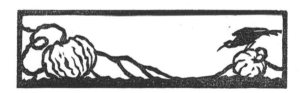

from 1992

Joshua Mertz contributed more stories to this book than any other author, and for good reason. His stories are consistently fun, varied in style, and often genuinely disturbing. (Just the thing for a cold October night!)

"The Demon's Wish" is something of a departure even from Joshua's usual broad range. Most of his stories begin with some idea, some frightening or fanciful notion that leads him down a creative pathway, but "The Demon's Wish" comes straight from the gut—a bitter examination of the folly and frailty of the human heart.

The Demon's Wish

by Joshua Mertz

I met him at an outdoor cafe somewhere up the California coast. Doesn't matter where. Summer day, warm breeze, sipping cappucino. Like that.

He was an odd bird; thick grey hair retaining hints of its former blondness, a gaunt but muscular frame under his cotton shirt, the lines of his tanned face indicating a lot of time spent with beetled brow. No different from hundreds of other used-to-be flower children littering the California sunscape. But there was something unique about him: a crazy air of intensity. He looked as if he had a story to tell. So I balanced my sandwich and cappucino over to his table and, God help me, invited myself into his presence.

Well, one thing led to another (you know how hot I am for a good anecdote), and I got him to talking, drawing darker and darker threads from his sad mouth. Until I came upon the hidden one. I guess he was aching to tell it.

"There was a woman," he began, then paused and looked down at his chewed fingernails. He cleared his throat. "There was a woman in my life once and I loved her more than...well, what can I say? More than life itself? More than Jesus loves the sinner? Certainly more than I should have.

"I won't even try to describe her. You fill in your own fantasy. Not a beauty queen. Not the perfect lips and the perfect hips, not the carnivorous smile and untouchable hair. But alive, you dig. Vibrantly, abundantly alive. She had the most incredible hazel eyes. Look right into your soul.

Happy, angry, expectant, whatever...she burned with life. Just burned with it.

"We lived together for a while. She told me she loved me for my sensitivity. It was great in the beginning. Then it got stormy. You know how it is. We made love. We argued. We thought about each other all the time. It was intense, let me tell you.

"I don't want to go into details, but I had some habits that she hated..."

He stopped here and extracted a pack of unfiltered Camels from his coat. He slid one out and lit it with practiced ease. In my mind's eye I saw his woman's face, somewhere in the past, wrinkle with disgust. He exhaled smoke, dragonlike, through his nose and continued.

"Maybe she was as scared as I was. It got worse. You know, the fights, the incriminations. She slept with my best friend and taunted me with it. Right at the end, I remember we went to one of those marriage encounter groups where you go out and camp together and try to work it out. We weren't married, but we went anyway.

"And we were lying together out under the stars on the last night. The final exercise was to tell each other where you pictured the two of you in five years. She pictured us still in the same house, married, maybe a couple of kids, doing those silly artistic things we liked to do.

"I told her that I did not picture us together at all. I told her I had decided to leave.

"She cried for awhile and wouldn't let me touch her. Then she got real quiet. That was the worst part. A month later I was gone, running as far as I could, staying with whoever would have me. I felt real free. For maybe two or three months.

"Then I began to phone. I wanted to get back together. She was leery. Once burned, you know. She got real cynical and I got real desperate and whiny. She started hanging out with a tough crowd, doing a lot of drugs, carrying a knife in her boot.

"She ended up marrying a biker. I mean a real biker. Pissed-on leather, chopped Harley, tattoos, the whole bit. Somebody told me she used to do the whole gang, but I couldn't allow myself to believe it. Nonetheless, I went over the edge. I was furious. I was crushed. I was outraged."

He dropped the butt of his Camel into the remains of his caffe latte and smiled an exceedingly bitter smile.

"Here it was me that ran away, and I was getting pissed about her dumping me for another man. Rich, eh? The epitome of irony. So I would phone her a lot and get real angry and ugly." He shook his head, looking at the table. "I began to fervently wish that she and her animal husband should die in some horrible motorcycle accident."

Another smile, this one much sadder, blew across his face.

"Gotta be careful what you wish for. They were on a back road near Tucson when a cow crossed the road and they hit it. She was flipped off the back of the Harley and hit headfirst against a tree. Smashed her skull in. Bikers don't wear helmets, you know. Died on the spot."

He sat in the warm California breeze for a bit, eyes unfocused. I said nothing. I thought he was done with his story, but he shook his head and smiled ironically.

"I don't talk about her much, but I did tell one guy once, when I was hitchhiking through somewhere. He was a good listener, much like you. He gave me this."

My storyteller placed an object on the table. It was a small bottle, less than a hand's breadth tall, made of opaque, iridescent glass such as one might find in a cheap antiquery. It was stoppered with a tiny cork and sealed with dark red wax. A faint, unpleasant musky odor came from the bottle. There appeared to be spidery handwriting on its pearlescent surface.

He was amused, in his wry way, with my interest. "It says 'Feed me blood and cry help.' Pretty twisted, eh?"

I nodded my head in mute agreement.

"You can keep it," he smiled. "As a gift."

Again, I said nothing and waited for him to continue.

"The guy told me that the bottle holds a teeny little demon who could grant me my fondest wish. I thought he was crazy. Just like you think I'm crazy.

"So I put it in my pocket and fondled it now and then and thought a lot about the teeny demon inside and about what my wish would be.

"Then one night, in the desert under the mad bright stars, I took out the cork, poked my finger with a knife, squeezed a drop of blood into the bottle, and said, 'Help.'"

By this time I was transfixed. He had me completely. I was expecting either some horrible punchline or a fabulous ghost story. I got neither.

"The demon turned out to be about two inches tall, looked a lot like a cartoon cockroach, and stunk to high hell. Just kind of sat on top of the bottle and kept asking me in this gravely little voice what my wish was.

"'I'm thinking,' I told it.

"It sneered. 'You been thinking about it for the last three months.'

"It was right, you know. I knew exactly what my wish was. And that little turd-colored thing told me I could always take it back. I didn't even have to take the traditional caution in stating my wish. It merely needed my vocal statement for legal purposes.

"I really did love her. Or at least I thought I did. Lately I've come to think that I merely wanted to possess her, like a car or a TV or something. Doesn't matter. I told the demon that I wanted her back. As if I had never left. I worded it very carefully, more for my own assurance than the demon's."

He paused again here to light another Camel. I virtually held my breath while his trembling hand put the burning match to the end of his cigarette.

"And—boom—there I was back in the kitchen of her house where we had once lived together. She was standing across the room, a little greyer, a little heavier, but alive again." He sighed, exhaling smoke. "Alive.

"I was stunned. My voice wouldn't work. We locked eyes.

"'Why did you do this to me?' she said.

"And I knew what she meant.

"You see, the demon had actually warped the fabric of reality so that I had literally never left her. I even had all the memories. I remembered the last night of the couples' encounter weekend. Remembered asking her to marry me that very same night, with the starlight pouring down like white honey. We had had the ceremony out in her back yard. I had gotten drunk.

"And there were all the years since. The memory of them flooded through me as I stood staring into her eyes. It had not been pretty. I had never quit smoking and she hated me for that. I hated her for hating me and turned to drinking. My son was frightened every time he smelled booze on my breath because he knew I would probably beat him. My woman was too strong to let me lay a hand on her. Even though I sometimes did. Two miscarriages. A long-term Valium addiction. Our daughter born retarded and abandoned to adoption.

"Some couples are strengthened by adversity. We were torn apart. Literally. She had a bleeding ulcer from living with me. I had become childish, unable to deal with the way her strength reflected the meanness of my soul. She became a nagging shrew, given to afternoon trysts with a faceless string of younger lovers.

"Standing there, staring at this wonderful woman I remembered with such avid love, my mind was awhirl with an acid storm of memories, a swarm of harpies that twisted at the rotten sinews of my soul. We had torn our holy bond apart with angry recriminations, petty revenges, and cruel, shunning silences.

"We had squandered our love like so much loose change, the sweetness of our hearts trapped in a doomed marriage, stifled and festering until that love had been transformed into a cancer that ate at our very marrow.

"It was hell.

"And she looked straight into my eyes, as strong as ever. Straight into my soul. And hated me for calling her back from her dreamless rest.

"I gripped the edge of the counter. It was sticky with a days-old spilled beer, my weapon of choice. 'I'm sorry,' I managed to stammer.

"Her voice was a whisper. 'I loved you once.'

It was the last thing I heard her say. I managed to pull my eyes from her terrible gaze and looked down at my hand gripping the counter. The demon stood on my white knuckles. It looked up at me with vicious mockery. 'Well?' it said.

"I told the demon to take it back. And it did.

"And she fell away from me, infinitely sad at our parting yet again. My heart cried out, and I was at one with her, flying through the air, and at the same time objectively outside, watching her forever sail in dreamy slow motion toward her crushing rendezvous with a tree. It is a vision that will stay with me until I die.

"Then I was back in the desert and it was night again by the campfire. The demon sat on the lip of its bottle, looking up at me.

"'You mortals are all the same,' it said. 'Never know when to leave well enough alone.'

"I cursed the demon until I was sobbing. Screamed all my pain at the stinking bug thing.

"'Listen, asshole,' the demon said. 'You made the wish, not me. So don't go calling me anything you can't say to a mirror.'

"Then it slipped back into the bottle and pulled the cork shut."

I left my sandwich and half my cappucino sitting on the table in the California sunshine. I never saw my storyteller again, and I count myself lucky for that. But occasionally, always late at night and often under the mad bright stars of the desert, I sit with the little bottle in one hand and a knife in the other. And I think about demons.

Carey Curtis Smith

Hannah of the Fields

from
1991

When you throw a ghost story party, there is one thing you hope for most of all: The Shivers. A sudden chill from listening. Hair standing up all along the scalp. The Shivers are very rare, and having written a lot of Halloween stories, I can tell you from experience they're very hard to achieve. That's why most people go for comedy, or straight horror, or adventure. The Shivers are, for most people, just too hard to invoke.

"Hannah of the Fields" gave me The Shivers when I first heard it. I think it's safe to say it did the same for everyone in the room that night. It's a quiet story of love and loss and autumn magic set in the nineteenth century, and it gets under the skin in just the right way.

I'm not surprised that Carey Smith is a master at summoning The Shivers. We've been friends since we met in high school drama class, and for several years we jointly hosted the most ambitious Halloween parties two teenagers ever attempted. After graduation, Carey moved to Redlands, California, where he became a local celebrity, garnering over 30 awards for his work as an actor and director in various local theaters, most notably for his staging of Dandelion Wine, adapted from the Ray Bradbury novel.

With all that to occupy him, Carey only rarely managed to come out to read at our parties. But when he did, he always brought The Shivers with him.

Hannah of the Fields

by Carey Curtis Smith

Papa was a handsome man but he never remarried. After Mama was buried beneath the cottonwood tree beyond the barn, Papa focused his passions on our farm. With magic hands tanned the color of red earth he coaxed the vines and crops from the fields. The house was tall and lean, and its whitewashed sideboards gleamed amidst his harvest of golden corn. But of all the recollections and faded memories I have of those early years in Oklahoma, I remember most our Hannah.

Hannah stood high in the center of the cornfield and surveyed our golden crop. She warded off the black crows and embraced the autumnal winds. She was born of cottonwood twigs, straw, burlap and Mama's old broom. Some thought it peculiar that we chose an old gingham dress and bonnet that once belonged to Mama to cover Hannah's wooden skeleton. But the effect was haunting. Hannah, named for a runaway who helped deliver me, stood tall in the field gazing over the husks and ears towards the house. At times, when the wind blew just so and the sun cast long purple shadows across the farmlands, it seemed as if our Hannah were actually waving at us or someone else not seen by us. Sometimes she gave the impression of a woman crying; lost in a tall green field, crying a helpless silent sound. Only the wind and the rustling of corn, like tumultuous applause, could be heard and many a night I pressed close to my window glass, straining to hear her nocturnal plea.

Papa never spoke of Hannah directly, but would dutifully change her garments according to the season. In winter, she wore black with a deep blue shawl and bonnet while in spring she wore green with a vivid yellow taffeta sash. In summer, red calico and in fall, plum, deep and rich, with a bodice of cream-colored lace. Oftentimes, Papa would stare high into the baking noonday sun and then leave me alone by the house only to return with a parasol or Japanese fan for Hannah. I followed him many times to that magic place in the center of the field. We waded through forests of scratching, rustling cornstalks which opened onto a clearing of packed loam. The area was devoid of corn but a profusion of pumpkins and vines littered the ground. At the center stood Hannah and it always seemed, as if suddenly bashful of Papa's handsome face and gray eyes, she would turn her burlap- and button-eyed face downward and her fan, held in stick fingers, fluttered in the breeze.

Many of the neighboring farmers' wives gossiped over clotheslines about Papa's eccentricity and further rumors commenced when Papa emptied two rounds of buckshot into the britches of the Thatcher boys as they attempted to steal poor Hannah from her lofty perch. Needless to say, all of this commotion over a scarecrow became the seeds of what were later to blossom into a variety of wild superstitious stories of to be told at hearthside to wide-eyed children.

Still, after years of observing and putting aside odd occurrences as coincidence or an over-active imagination, I was increasingly aware, in spite of myself, of something unexplainable. Papa had grown more stoic and distant as the years went by and our relationship more strained. I often wished he would remarry in order that I might have another soul to converse with. I often voiced these concerns to Mama. I'd kneel beside her modest grave, clear away the leaves and deposit a handful of cornflower blossoms on the

spot. The tall cottonwoods above would sway and whisper quietly to me. This was my only communion with the mother I never knew, and I often wished to feel the soft touch of her gentle hands or hear the music in her laughter. I knew, for black Hannah told me, that in many ways I was like Mama and perhaps this explained Papa's increasing silence and distance.

Black Hannah—she had no other name—was a runaway headed north to Canada when she stumbled onto our farm. Mama and Papa did not share the Southern sympathies regarding runaways and thus Hannah became a closely guarded secret. She lived in the barn and remained unknown until the howling October night when I was born. That night Mama's life was carried away with the autumn leaves and mine began. It was Hannah who cradled me in ebony hands while Papa buried his face and wept into Mama's dark hair.

Three years later (Hannah had been secreted into Northern safety), Papa decided to make a scarecrow. A scarecrow which I endowed with the loving appellation, Hannah of the Fields, in memory of the only mother I had known.

Beyond our house and bordering the long dirt road to our farm ran a row of cottonwoods. Like giant leafy sentinels, they acted as a barrier to prevent the winds from carrying off precious topsoil and many a dust storm circumscribed our farm because of those cottonwoods. Black Hannah used to say that the trees also trapped the souls of those who had passed from this world. At night you could hear their mournful cries in the high branches. As a small child I often wished that Mama's soul had been trapped that October night and might be shaken down but I was always too frightened to climb into those haunted branches.

One night, not long before the harvest, I was awakened by what I thought to be a cobweb across my face. It startled me to sitting upright in the darkness of my attic room. Only the orange moon cast its light upon my window. And then I heard, quite clearly, my name. It was whispered and seemed to come from all directions. It was whispered again, and ever so faintly I smelled cornflower mixed with fragrances of harvest. I crept softly toward my window and gazed down upon the endless acres of waving corn which rippled golden in the moon's glow.

There stood Papa, eyes staring upward at Hannah, and her skirts rustled in the wind. Slowly, Papa reached upward and touched stick fingers. The wind blew and cloud shadows danced across the moon and yet it seemed that for a brief moment I beheld two lovers in their embrace; but as the clouds moved on and leaves quietly deposited themselves on the porch, only Hannah the scarecrow remained.

In the distance I could make out Papa's tall slim silhouette walking towards the barn. A lantern attached to the barn door swung crazily in the wind. Papa stood for a moment in its light and even at that distance I could see that his piercing gray eyes were wet with tears. He disappeared inside, and seconds later a shot rang out clear in the October night.

I bolted from my room, choking in horror and fear. A sickness washed over me as I ran for the cornfield and the barn beyond. I stumbled, tasting dirt, and, tangling in pumpkin creepers, struggled to break free and ran on again. I reached the clearing and stopped. Hannah was dancing. Under the round October moon she spun. In moon shadows her gingham skirts swept the dust and shushed and rustled amid the swaying cornstalks. The corn rows bowed like lanky schoolboys hoping to have the next waltz. How they would bow low in the winds! But Hannah paid them no mind; she whirled past, leaving only darkness, dust and the smell of harvest perfumes. All the fields sighed in the night winds and the moon shone red, red as the blood sprayed on the barn door, as Hannah danced.

Mama's sister had taken me in after that October night and I was to leave forever the Oklahoma farm, with its rows of waving corn and sentries of cottonwoods ensnared with lost souls. I returned only once in my adulthood to see the old homestead and note the modern improvements. What struck me as odd was that Hannah remained fluttering in her bonnet at the center of the cornfield. Perhaps the new owners enjoyed the air of mystery and folklore that surrounded her.

Beside her swayed another scarecrow in farmer's overalls much like the ones my Papa once wore; a straw hat was cocked to one side of its burlap face with gray button eyes. And when the wind blew just so and the long purple shadows of the setting sun stretched across the fields, it appeared, to some, as if stick fingers intertwined and as the corn bowed in the wind, Hannah and her gray-eyed partner danced.

Michael Mayhew and Joshua Mertz

AFTERWORD

AFTERWORD

On Throwing a Halloween Story Party

by Michael Mayhew and Joshua Mertz

When we began this book, one of the issues we wrestled with was the extent to which *Harvest Tales* ought to be about the parties from which it was born. In and of themselves, the parties were very special and we are particularly proud of the fact that our parties inspired at least two other groups to throw similar bashes. On the other hand, the Play's the thing—or in our case, the Stories are. Party-throwing minutiae are not for everybody. Hence this Afterword: a few notes for interested readers about how we organized the parties that produced the stories in this book.

BACKGROUND

In 1986, the two of us lived down the street from each other near the University of Southern California, where we attended film school. We discovered in each other a mutual love of Halloween, and one October we reminisced about the Halloweens we had enjoyed when we were younger. Michael was a veteran of many years of Halloween parties, most of them team efforts with Carey Smith; Joshua, having traveled a great deal in his life, described parties he had attended in locales ranging from San Francisco to Yuma, Arizona.

It was out of these conversations that the basic idea for the story party emerged. Wouldn't it be fun, we thought, to co-host a party to which each of the guests brought an original Halloween tale? We knew lots of talented people at school—what could be simpler? We set about making invitations.

That first party was a full-fledged costume party with twenty-five or thirty guests, but which netted a disappointing three stories: one each from the two hosts, and one from Carey Smith. But it was also a huge amount of fun, a tremendous learning experience, and it set a number of precedents for the way the rest of the parties would be run—teaching us the first of many lessons about what does and does not work for a story party.

Lesson Number One is that a Halloween party should be either a costume party or a story party, but not both. The reasons for this are: 1) sitting and listening to stories gets a bit uncomfortable in a costume, and 2) costume parties want to be boisterous, whereas story parties involve a lot of listening and need more room to breathe.

In the years that followed, we refined the concept to a very specific potluck dinner and evening of stories, and at the same time tried to reinvent aspects of the party each year so it wouldn't get stale. The size of the gatherings fluctuated enormously. The third year there were only two stories and four guests (one of our favorite years, actually); the fifth year there were fifteen stories and about thirty-five guests.

GUESTS

To throw a story party you have to have friends who enjoy listening to stories. That's it. Writing skills are not a prerequisite. It's perfectly possible to get together and read Halloween classics. It is a lot of fun and makes for a good party.[1]

To throw a party with *original* stories, however, requires another kind of guest—those who like to write.

Artists, musicians, poets, *raconteurs*, that guy at the office who always talks about how he's going to write—even the quiet intern in the mailroom—are all potential authors for a story party. Finding them is key—not everybody is into this—then all you have to do is persuade them to write a story and read it aloud at a party.

Lesson Number Two: the world is full of creative, talented writers who would rather crawl under a rock than write a story, much less read it aloud to a roomful of people. To get people to write and attend the party you have to bug them.

A lot.

Invitations to write usually went out in mid-September. This to make sure the invitees had at least a month in which to crank out a story. In point of fact, most of the stories were written in the forty-eight hours prior to the party. But the thirty-day notice eliminated the "I didn't have enough time" excuse.

Here's a typical invitation:

> It's that time again.
>
> Or it will be soon. October. Probably you haven't recovered from your Labor Day sunburn, but that's irrelevant. Time is swift. Already the mornings are cool again. Give it a month and the air will be crisp, and the sky orange and smoky at twilight.
>
> October is coming. The time for stories. You're invited...
>
> Specifically, you are invited to write a story, 2,500 words or fewer, and then read it aloud on Halloween night at the home of Joshua Mertz. Your story should relate to Hallowe'en in some way. What way is up to you. It can be any genre. It can be as funny or sad or frightening as you can make it, so long as it ties in with some aspect of Hallowe'en...

Lesson Number Three: Notice the invitation contains an upper limit on length; if you do not impose an upper limit on story length, someone is going to bring in his novel-in-progress. Twenty-five hundred words is a very good length for a story. That's about twelve or so double-spaced pages and usually takes under fifteen minutes to read. After about fifteen minutes an audience begins to want something new.

After the writing invitations had been sent out, we would send out one or more "reminder" invitations, as well as make annoying phone calls to the potential authors. Remember, silent trust results in a lot fewer stories than pestering and nagging.

Finally, an official invitation to the party was sent out to everyone we wanted to attend, writers and audience alike. It's a lot of invitations for one party, but it pays off in the quality of the gathering.

STORIES

Generally "Halloween" was enough of a theme to inspire stories every year, but a couple of times we experimented with other rules and the results were instructional. One year we specifically asked the authors to write a "ghost story," because we thought it was an aspect of the genre that was not receiving enough attention and besides, we were interested in what everyone thought about ghosts. There was not a single ghost story that year.

People ignore rules, especially when they pertain to parties. Keep in mind that the maxim "rules are made to be broken" dates back to the Pleistocene. Personal challenges work best. Better to goad your participants individually than to issue a blanket edict. Call people and ask if they have any story ideas they'd like to discuss. Be their counselor. Remind them of the approaching deadline. The only rule of writing should be the length limit. And even that rule can be broken sometimes.

FOOD

At our parties, the stories were only half the evening. Food was absolutely integral to the festivities. In fact, the official name of the party was The Post Autumnal Equinox Ghost Story Reading and Pot-Luck Dinner.

And *such* food! Roast pork with garlic and smoked duck and stir-fried vegetables! Fresh Caesar salad and thick carrot soup! Corn chowder and shrimp bisque and lasagna and rigatoni with pesto and spicy chicken ravioli and grilled sausage and whipped sweet potatoes! Pumpkin pie and apple flan torte, bread pudding and Black Forest cake! The story party became an unofficial start to the holiday season of eating. A sort of pre-Thanksgiving autumn feast, but without the locked-in mandate of turkey.

The tricky part was managing the pot-luck signups so there would be enough food for everyone and not too much of any one thing (eleven deserts, say, and one entree). The food strategy we adopted was to provide some sort of "anchor meal," like a roast, some mashed potatoes, a couple of liters of soft drinks, some Halloween candy, maybe some beer—not enough to feed the crowd by any stretch, but a reliable core of food so that, no matter what else came in over the transom and no matter how late some of the dishes arrived, we would be able to serve the early guests something tasty.

So Lesson Number Four is: Good food is the backbone of a good story party. A contented stomach and a houseful of good cooking smells help put people in the mood to listen. Visiting and laughing together over dinner make it easier for the writers to read in front of people—it is no longer a room full of strangers, but an audience of friends.

DECORATIONS

When you are throwing a Halloween party for adults, the way you decorate goes a long way to setting the tone of the evening. There is a fine line between creating an atmosphere of spooky, brooding fun and making everyone feel that they wandered into a kiddie party by mistake.

Start with simple black candles. They don't cost a lot and they go a long way toward setting a mood. Invest in a bolt of cheap black cloth. You can use it as bunting over windows and doorways, as a tablecloth, or to decorate a railing, among many other applications—a high mileage item. Plaster skulls work, and the stretchy cobwebs they sell at the dime store are also very good. Be very selective with any store-bought decorations, though. Most dime store decorations are designed *not to frighten children.* Sometimes that's just the ticket, but be forewarned—a little goofiness goes a long way when your goal is to put a group of adults in the mood to sit together and read Halloween stories. You may want one or two special items that make the party uniquely yours.

The best decorations, of course, are jack-o'-lanterns. There is something magic about putting a candle into a carved pumpkin. Even a sloppy jack-o'-lantern seems alive when the lights are low. They invoke childhood feelings without seeming childish. We averaged about twenty-five (25!) jack-o'-lanterns. If you shop around in the last weeks before Halloween you can usually find a store selling pumpkins at cost to lure people in. Use the cheap child-safe pumpkin carving tools you'll find in the grocery store. Not only are they safe, but they work much better than kitchen knives.

Around the sixth year we invited the guests earlier and let each person carve his own jack-o'-lantern. In addition to saving us a lot of carving work (and the attendant wrist cramps), this ended up serving as a terrific icebreaker. The resulting rogue's gallery of carved gourds was a wonderful reflection of the personalities at the party.

The last few years we took that notion to another level, inviting several guests to bring works of art in the same way we had invited others to write. The resulting decorations were wonderful, ranging from Day of the Dead altars to expressionistic paintings to charcoal sketches to carefully arranged dead flowers.

One final element is music. We made a long tape of our favorite Halloween-themed music, from classics like *Danse Macabre* to Tom Waits's *Black Rider*, which we played in a loop through the duration of the evening.[2]

In later years, by using several portable stereos, we created pools of sound in different rooms. Guests arriving might hear thunder and rain in the entry hall, organ music in the living room, frogs croaking in the bathroom, monks chanting in the hallway, and so on.

PROGRAMMING

The Post Autumnal Equinox Ghost Story Reading and Pot-Luck Dinner unfolds like a story. Or a menu. The food and stories are alternated thusly:

◆ Guests arrive and spend and hour with drinks, appetizers, and conversation;

◆ around seven, serve the entrees buffet-style;

◆ after dinner, begin reading stories until through half of them;

◆ break for desserts, coffee, and more talk;

◆ read the second half of the stories;

◆ say good night with a shiver.

One of the fun parts of hosting a story party is getting to choose what order the stories will be read in. If you have a reliably strong reader who is an entertaining writer, let him or her read first to get the evening off to a lively start. Beyond that, when each writer arrived with a story we would collect it from him or her and ask the question, "Is it more a funny story or a serious story?" Then we would attempt to arrange the stories funny, serious, funny, serious, doing our best to ensure that the strongest writers were distributed throughout the evening.

Of great importance was the Reader's Chair, the focal point of the party. It was always the biggest, most comfortable chair in whoever's house we were using. Beside the Chair was a reading lamp and a small table to keep a glass of water or a cup of coffee on. And something else—some small, odd decoration that said Halloween.

ON READING ALOUD

Remain calm. Whether you are reading your own story or someone else's, there are a few simple rules to remember.

Above all, know your material. Read through it to yourself—aloud—ahead of time. Feel free to make marks on it for what to emphasize, when to pause, when to breathe. Do not rush. This is a snazzed-up parlor game, not a speed-reading contest. You usually cannot hear how fast you are reading, so consciously slow down. Give each word its weight, its due, then let it slip past like sand through your fingers or a handful of pebbles on a walk. Do not be afraid to pause. Pauses are essential to good storytelling.

Speak up. Do not shout, but speak in a firm voice that the whole room might hear you. Sit up moderately straight (like your Mother always told you to do). It is important that your spine be aligned up and down in order to run your lungs and speaking machinery at maximum efficiency.

It is good to have only the reading light on and the room lights dim. This allows you to concentrate on the reading of the story and forget about the audience. But do look up from the text now and then. Audiences like that sort of thing.

Know your material, enjoy the flow of the language, and sit up straight. Halloween lives in you and is dying to get out. Let it out.

NOTES

1. Classic Halloween story recommendations: *The October Country* and *Long After Midnight*, short story collections by Ray Bradbury; *Bloodcurdling Tales of Horror and the Macabre*, a collection of H.P. Lovecraft stories; "Flop Sweat" by Harlan Ellison (in the *Shatterday* collection); "Harry" by Rosemary Timperly and "Ringing the Changes" by Robert Aickman (in *Roald Dahl's Book of Ghost Stories*); "The Love Letter" by Jack Finney (in *I Love Galesburg in the Springtime*); "The Highwayman" by Alfred Noyes.

2. Halloween music suggestions: *A Night On Bald Mountain* (in particular, the Leopold Stokowski orchestration of this Mussorgsky classic—the one used in Disney's *Fantasia*); *Danse Macabre*, by Camille Saint-Saëns (Op. 40); "Dream of a Witches' Sabbath" (the fifth movement of Berlioz's *Symphony Fantastique*); J.S. Bach's *Toccata and Fugue in D Minor* (BWV 565); the movie soundtracks from *Dracula* (John Williams's version), *Psycho*, *Cat People*, *A Clockwork Orange*, *Nightmare Before Christmas* (especially "This Is Halloween"); Sinead O' Connor's "I Am Stretched On Your Grave"; Tom Waits's album *Black Rider*.

Harvest Tales & Midnight Revels

was typeset on an Apple® Macintosh® computer in ITC Galliard®, a typeface with appropriately Gothic stylistic overtones. Happily, no Microsoft® products were used in the design or production of this book. Bald Mountain Books thanks you for your patronage.